W9-BNM-855

**V'S
ROBOT CITY™**

ISAAC ASIMOV'S

ROBOT CITY

™

BOOK 4: PRODIGY

ARTHUR BYRON COVER

A Byron Preiss Visual Publications, Inc. Book

ACE BOOKS, NEW YORK

This book is an Ace original edition, and has never been
previously published.

ISAAC ASIMOV'S ROBOT CITY
BOOK 4: PRODIGY

An Ace Book/published by arrangement with
Byron Preiss Visual Publications, Inc.

PRINTING HISTORY
Ace edition/January 1988

ISBN: 0-441-37384-4

Ace Books are published by The Berkley Publishing Group,
200 Madison Avenue, New York, New York 10016.
The name "ACE" and the "A" logo are
trademarks belonging to Charter Communications, Inc.
PRINTED IN THE UNITED STATES OF AMERICA

10 9 8 7 6 5 4 3 2 1

CONTENTS

THE SENSE OF HUMOR
ISAAC ASIMOV

Would a robot feel a yearning to be human?

You might answer that question with a counter-question. Does a Chevrolet feel a yearning to be a Cadillac?

The counter-question makes the unstated comment that a machine has no yearnings.

But the very point is that a robot is not quite a machine, at least in potentiality. A robot is a machine that is made as much like a human being as it is possible to make it, and somewhere there may be a boundary line that may be crossed.

We can apply this to life. An earthworm doesn't yearn to be a snake; a hippopotamus doesn't yearn to be an elephant. We have no reason to think such creatures are self-conscious and dream of something more than they are. Chimpanzees and gorillas seem to be self-aware, but we have no reason to think that they yearn to be human.

A human being, however, dreams of an afterlife and yearns to become one of the angels. Somewhere, life crossed a boundary line. At some point a species arose that was not only aware of itself but had the capacity to be dissatisfied with itself.

Perhaps a similar boundary line will someday be crossed in the construction of robots.

But if we grant that a robot might someday aspire to humanity, in what way would he so aspire? He might aspire to the possession of the legal and social status that human beings are born to. That was the theme of my story "The Bicentennial Man" (1976), and in his pursuit of such status, my robot-hero was willing to give up all his robotic qualities, one by one, right down to his immortality.

That story, however, was more philosophical than realistic. What is there about a human being that a robot might properly envy—what human physical or mental *characteristic?* No sensible robot would envy human fragility, or human incapacity to withstand mild changes in the environment, or human need for sleep, or aptitude for the trivial mistake, or tendency to infectious and degenerative disease, or incapacitation through illogical storms of emotion.

He might, more properly, envy the human capacity for friendship and love, his wide-ranging curiosity, his eagerness for experience. I would like to suggest, though, that a robot who yearned for humanity might well find that what he would most want to understand, and most frustratingly *fail* to understand, would be the human sense of humor.

The sense of humor is by no means universal among human beings, though it does cut across all cultures. I have known many people who didn't laugh, but who looked at you in puzzlement or perhaps disdain if you tried to be funny. I need go no further than my father, who routinely shrugged off my cleverest sallies as unworthy of the attention of a serious man. (Fortunately, my mother laughed at all my jokes, and most uninhibitedly, or I might have grown up emotionally stunted.)

The curious thing about the sense of humor, however, is that, as far as I have observed, no human being will *admit* to its lack. People might admit they hate dogs and dislike children, they might cheerfully own up to cheating on their income tax or on their marital partner as a matter of right, and might not object to being considered inhumane or dishonest, through the simple expediency of switching adjectives and calling themselves realistic or businesslike.

However, accuse them of lacking a sense of humor and they will deny it hotly every time, no matter how openly and how often they display such a lack. My father, for instance, always maintained that he had a keen sense of humor and would prove it as soon as he heard a joke worth laughing at (though he never did, in my experience).

Why, then, do people object to being accused of humor-lessness? My theory is that people recognize (subliminally, if not openly) that a sense of humor is typically human, more so than any other characteristic, and refuse demotion to sub-humanity.

Only once did I take up the matter of a sense of humor in a science-fiction story, and that was in my story "Jokester," which first appeared in the December, 1956 issue of *Infinity Science Fiction* and which was most recently reprinted in my collection *The Best Science Fiction of Isaac Asimov* (Doubleday, 1986).

The protagonist of the story spent his time telling jokes to a computer (I quoted six of them in the course of the story). A computer, of course, is an immobile robot; or, which is the same thing, a robot is a mobile computer; so the story deals with robots and jokes. Unfortunately, the problem in the story for which a solution was sought was *not* the nature of humor, but the source of all the jokes one hears. And there is an answer, too, but you'll have to read the story for that.

However, I don't just write science fiction. I write what-ever it falls into my busy little head to write, and (by some undeserved stroke of good fortune) my various publishers are under the weird impression that it is illegal not to publish any manuscript I hand them. (You can be sure that I never disabuse them of this ridiculous notion.)

Thus, when I decided to write a joke book, I did, and Houghton-Mifflin published it in 1971 under the title of *Isaac Asimov's Treasury of Humor.* In it, I told 640 jokes that I happened to have as part of my memorized repertoire. (I also have enough for a sequel to be entitled *Isaac Asimov Laughs Again*, but I can't seem to get around to writing it no matter how long I sit at the keyboard and how quickly I manipulate the keys.) I interspersed those jokes with my own theories concerning what is funny and how one makes what is funny even funnier.

Mind you, there are as many different theories of humor

as there are people who write on the subject, and no two theories are alike. Some are, of course, much stupider than others, and I felt no embarrassment whatever in adding my own thoughts on the subject to the general mountain of commentary.

It is my feeling, to put it as succinctly as possible, that the one necessary ingredient in every successful joke is a sudden alteration in point of view. The more radical the alteration, the more suddenly it is demanded, the more quickly it is seen, the louder the laugh and the greater the joy.

Let me give you an example with a joke that is one of the few I made up myself:

Jim comes into a bar and finds his best friend, Bill, at a corner table gravely nursing a glass of beer and wearing a look of solemnity on his face. Jim sits down at the table and says sympathetically, "What's the matter, Bill?"

Bill sighs, and says, "My wife ran off yesterday with my best friend."

Jim says, in a shocked voice, "What are you talking about, Bill? I'm your best friend."

To which Bill answers softly, "Not anymore."

I trust you see the change in point of view. The natural supposition is that poor Bill is sunk in gloom over a tragic loss. It is only with the last three words that you realize, quite suddenly, that he is, in actual fact, delighted. And the average human male is sufficiently ambivalent about his wife (however beloved she might be) to greet this particular change in point of view with delight of his own.

Now, if a robot is designed to have a brain that responds to logic only (and of what use would any other kind of robot brain be to humans who are hoping to employ robots for their own purposes?), a sudden change in point of view would be hard to achieve. It would imply that the rules of logic were wrong in the first place or were capable of a flexibility that they obviously don't have. In addition, it would be dangerous to build ambivalence into a robot brain.

What we want from him is decision and not the to-be-or-not-to-be of a Hamlet.

Imagine, then, telling a robot the joke I have just given you, and imagine the robot staring at you solemnly after you are done, and questioning you, thus.

Robot: "But why is Jim no longer Bill's best friend? You have not described Jim as doing anything that would cause Bill to be angry with him or disappointed in him."

You: "Well, no, it's not that Jim has done anything. It's that someone else has done something for Bill that was so wonderful, that he has been promoted over Jim's head and has instantly become Bill's new best friend."

Robot: "But who has done this?"

You: "The man who ran away with Bill's wife, of course."

Robot (after a thoughtful pause): "But that can't be so. Bill must have felt profound affection for his wife and a great sadness over her loss. Is that not how human males feel about their wives, and how they would react to their loss?"

You: "In theory, yes. However, it turns out that Bill strongly disliked his wife and was *glad* someone had run off with her."

Robot (after another thoughtful pause): "But you did not say that was so."

You: "I know. That's what makes it funny. I led you in one direction and then suddenly let you know that was the wrong direction."

Robot: "Is it funny to mislead a person?"

You (giving up): "Well, let's get on with building this house."

In fact, some jokes actually depend on the illogical responses of human beings. Consider this one:

The inveterate horseplayer paused before taking his place at the betting windows, and offered up a fervent prayer to his Maker.

"Blessed Lord," he murmured with mountain-moving sincerity, "I know you don't approve of my gambling, but just this once, Lord, just this once, *please* let me break even. I need the money so badly."

If you were so foolish as to tell this joke to a robot, he would immediately say, "But to break even means that he would leave the races with precisely the amount of money he had when he entered. Isn't that so?"

"Yes, that's so."

"Then if he needs the money so badly, all he need do is not bet at all, and it would be just as though he had broken even."

"Yes, but he has this unreasoning need to gamble."

"You mean even if he loses."

"Yes."

"But that makes no sense."

"But the point of the joke is that the gambler doesn't understand this."

"You mean it's funny if a person lacks any sense of logic and is possessed of not even the simplest understanding?"

And what can you do but turn back to building the house again?

But tell me, is this so different from dealing with the ordinary humorless human being? I once told my father this joke:

Mrs. Jones, the landlady, woke up in the middle of the night because there were strange noises outside her door. She looked out, and there was Robinson, one of her boarders, forcing a frightened horse up the stairs.

She shrieked, "What are you doing, Mr. Robinson?"

He said, "Putting the horse in the bathroom."

"For goodness sake, why?"

"Well, old Higginbotham is such a wise guy. Whatever I tell him, he answers, 'I know. I know,' in such a superior way. Well, in the morning, he'll go to the bathroom and he'll come out yelling, 'There's a *horse* in the bathroom.' And I'll yawn and say, 'I know, I know.'"

* * *

And what was my father's response? He said, "Isaac, Isaac. You're a city boy, so you don't understand. You can't push a horse up the stairs if he doesn't want to go."

Personally, I thought that was funnier than the joke.

Anyway, I don't see why we should particularly want a robot to have a sense of humor, but the point is that the robot himself might want to have one—and how do we give it to him?

CHAPTER 1
CAN YOU FEEL ANYTHING
WHEN I DO THIS?

"Mandelbrot, what does it feel like to be a robot?"

"Forgive me, Master Derec, but that question is meaning-less. While it is certainly true that robots can be said to experience sensations vaguely analogous to specified human emotions in some respects, we lack feelings in the accepted sense of the word."

"Sorry, old buddy, but I can't help getting the hunch that you're just equivocating with me."

"That would be impossible. The very foundations of pos-itronic programming insist that robots invariably state the facts explicitly."

"Come, come, don't you concede it's possible that the differences between human and robotic perception may be, by and large, semantic? You agree, don't you, that many human emotions are simply the by-products of chemical re-actions that ultimately affect the mind, influencing moods and perceptions. You must admit, humans are nothing if not at the mercy of their bodies."

"That much has been proven, at least to the satisfaction of respected authorities."

"Then, by analogy, your own sensations are merely by-products of smoothly running circuitry and engine joints. A spaceship may feel the same way when, its various parts all working at peak efficiency, it breaks into hyperspace. The only difference between you and it being, I suppose, that you have a mind to perceive it."

Mandelbrot paused, his integrals preoccupied with sorting Derec's perspectives on these matters into several categories in his memory circuits. "I have never quite analyzed the problem that way before, Master Derec. But it seems that in many respects the comparison between human and robot, robot and spaceship must be exceedingly apt."

"Let's look at it this way, Mandelbrot. As a human, I am a carbon-based life-form, the superior result of eons of evolution of inferior biological life-forms. I know what it feels like because I have a mind to perceive the gulf between man and other species of animal life. And with careful, selective comparison, I can imagine—however minimally—what a lower life-form might experience as it makes its way through the day. Furthermore, I can communicate to others what I think it feels like."

"My logic circuits can accept this."

"Okay then, through analogy or metaphor or through a story I can explain to others what a worm, or a rat, or a cat, or even a dinosaur must feel as they hunt meat, go to sleep, sniff flowers, or whatever."

"I have never seen one of these creatures and certainly wouldn't presume to comprehend what it must be like to be one."

"Ah! But you *would* know—through proper analogy— what it must be like to be a spaceship."

"Possibly, but I have not been provided with the necessary programming to retrieve the information. Furthermore, I cannot see how such knowledge could possibly help me fulfill the behavioral standards implicit in the Three Laws."

"But you have been programmed to retrieve such information, and your body often reacts accordingly, and sometimes adversely, with regards to your perceptions."

"You are speaking theoretically?"

"Yes."

"Are you formally presenting me with a problem?"

"Yes."

"Naturally I shall do my best to please you, Master Derec, but my curiosity and logic integrals are only equipped to deal with certain kinds of problems. The one you appear to be presenting may be too subjective for my programmed potentials."

"Isn't all logic abstract, and hence somewhat subjective, at least in approach? You must agree that, through mutually agreed upon paths of logic, you can use the certain knowledge of two irrefutable facts to learn a third, equally irrefutable fact."

"Of course."

"Then can't you use such logic to reason how it might feel to be a spaceship, or any other piece of sufficiently advanced machinery?"

"Since you phrase it that manner, of course, but I fail to comprehend what benefit such an endeavor may bring me—or you."

Derec shrugged. It was night in Robot City. He and Mandelbrot had been out walking. He had felt the need to stretch his muscles after a long day spent studying some of the problems complicating his escape from this isolated planet. But at the moment they were sitting atop a rectangular tower and staring at the stars. "Oh, I don't know if it would be of any benefit, except perhaps to satisfy my curiosity. It just seems to me that you must have some idea of what it is like to be a robot, even if you don't have the means to express it."

"Such knowledge would require language, and such a language has not yet been invented."

"Hmmm. I suppose."

"However, I have just made an association that may be of some value."

"What's that?"

"Whenever you or Mistress Ariel have had no need of my assistance, I have been engaging in communication with the robots of this city. They haven't been wondering what it means or feels like to be a robot, but they have been devoting a tremendous amount of spare mental energy to the dilemma of what it must be like to be a human."

"Yes, that makes sense, after a fashion. The robots' goal

of determining the Laws of Humanics has struck me as a unique phenomenon."

"Perhaps it is not, Master Derec. After all, if I may remind you, you recall only your experiences of the last few weeks, and my knowledge of history is rather limited in scope. Even so, I never would have thought of making connections the way you have, which leads my circuits to conclude your subconscious is directing our conversation so that it has some bearing on your greater problems."

Derec laughed uncomfortably. He hadn't considered it before. Strange, he thought, that a robot had. "My subconscious? Perhaps. I suppose I feel that if I better understand the world I'm in, I might better understand myself."

"I believe I am acting in accordance with the Three Laws if I help a human know himself better. For that reason, my circuits are currently humming with a sensation you might recognize as pleasure."

"That's nice. Now if you'll excuse me, I'd like to be alone right now." For a moment Derec felt a vague twinge of anxiety, and he actually feared that he might be insulting Mandelbrot, a robot that, after all they'd been through together, he couldn't help but regard as his good friend.

But if Mandelbrot had taken umbrage, he showed no evidence of it. He was, as always, inscrutable. "Of course. I shall wait in the lobby."

Derec watched as Mandelbrot walked to the lift and slowly descended. Of course Mandelbrot hadn't taken umbrage. It was impossible for him to be insulted.

Crossing his legs to be more comfortable, Derec returned to looking at the stars and the cityscape spread out below and beyond, but his thoughts remained inward. Normally he was not the reflective type, but tonight he felt moody, and gave in easily to the anxiousness and insecurity he normally held in check while trying to deal with his various predicaments more logically.

He smiled at this observation on what he was feeling. Perhaps he was taking himself too seriously, the result of lately reading too much Shakespeare. He had discovered the plays of the ancient, so-called "Immortal Bard" as a means of mental escape and relaxation. Now he was finding that the more he scrutinized the texts, the more he learned about himself. It was as if the specific events and characters portrayed in the plays spoke directly to him, and had some immediate bearing on the situation in which he had found himself when he had awakened, shorn of memory, in that survival pod not so long ago.

He couldn't help but wonder why the plays were beginning to affect him so. It was as if he was beginning to redefine himself through them.

He shrugged again, and again pondered the stars. Not just to analyze them for clues to the location of the world he was on, but to respond to them as he imagined countless men and women had throughout the course of history. He tried to imagine how they had looked to the men of Shakespeare's time, before mankind had learned how the universe came to be, where the Earth stood in relation to it, or how to build a hyperspace drive. Their searching but scientifically ignorant minds must have perceived in the stars a coldly savage beauty beyond the range of his empathy.

One star in the sky, perhaps, might be the sun of his homeworld. Somewhere out there, he thought, someone knew the answers to his questions. Someone who knew who he really was and how he came to be in that survival pod.

Below him was the city of towers, pyramids, cubes, spires and tetragons, some of which, even as he watched, were changing in accordance with the city's program. Occasionally robots, their activity assisting the alterations and additions, glistened in the reflections of the starlight reflected in turn from the city walls. The robots never slept, the city never slept. It changed constantly, unpredictably.

The city was like a giant robot, composed of billions upon billions of metallic cells functioning in accordance to nuclei-encoded DNA patterns of action and reaction. Although composed of inorganic matter, the city was a living thing, a triumph of a design philosophy Derec called "minimalist engineering."

Derec had partially been inspired to ascend to the top of this tower—through a door and lift that appeared when he needed them—precisely because he had watched its basic structure coil, snakelike, from the street like a giant, growing ribbon. And once the ribbon had reached its preordained height, the cells had spread out and coalesced into a solid structure. Perhaps they had multiplied as well.

Two towers directly in front of him merged and sank into the street as if dropping on a great lift. About a kilometer away to his right, a set of buildings of varying heights gradually became uniform, then merged into a single, vast, square construction. It stayed that way for approximately three minutes, then methodically began metamorphosing into a row of crystals.

A few days ago, such a sight would have instilled within him a sense of wonder. Now it was all very ordinary. No wonder he had sought to amuse himself by engaging in what he had thought was a slight mental diversion.

Suddenly a tremendous glare appeared in the midst of the city. Derec averted his eyes in panic, assuming it was an explosion.

But as the seconds passed and the glare remained, he realized that no sound or sensation of violence had accompanied its birth. Whatever its nature, its presence had been declared as if it had been turned on by a switch.

Feeling a little self-conscious, he slowly removed his fingers from his eyes and ventured a look. The glare was coalescing into a series of easily definable colors. Various hues of crimson, ochre, and blue. The colors changed as the tetragonal pyramid they were coming from changed.

The pyramid was situated near the city's border. The eight-sided figure was balanced precariously on the narrow tip of its base, and it rotated like a spinning top in slow motion. From Derec's vantage point it resembled a tremendous bauble, thanks to those brilliantly changing lights.

Watching it, he gradually felt all anxieties cease. His own problems seemed dwarfed into insignificance compared to the splendor of this sight. What beauty this city was capable of!

Soon this feeling of calm was uprooted by his growing curiosity, a restless need to know more that quickly became overwhelming, relentlessly gnawing. He would have to examine the building firsthand, then return to his "roost" where his access controls were, and get down to seriously plumbing the depths of the city's mysterious programming.

Like the plays of Shakespeare, the strange structure seemed a good place to escape to for a time. Besides, he never knew—he might find out something that would help him and Ariel get off this crazy planet.

"So there you are!" said a familiar voice behind him. "What are you doing here?"

He looked up to see Ariel staring down at him. She stood with her legs apart and her hands on her hips. The breeze blew strands of hair across her nose and mouth. She had a mischievous light in her eyes. Suddenly it was time to forget the city for a moment and to stare at her. Her unexpected presence had taken his breath away. His nerves had come back.

All right, he admitted to himself, *so it's not just her presence—it's* her—*everything about her!*

"Hi. I was just thinking of you," he managed to say, the catch in his voice painfully obvious, at least to him.

"Liar," she said with combined sarcasm and warmth. "But that's all right. I wanted to see you, too."

"Have you noticed that building?"

"Of course. I've been standing here for the last few moments, while you've been zoned out. Amazing, isn't it? I bet you're already trying to figure out how to analyze it."

"Oh, of course. How did you find me?" he asked.

"Wolruf sniffed you out. She and Mandelbrot are waiting downstairs."

"What's Wolruf doing down there?"

"She doesn't like the cold air up here. Says it makes her too nostalgic for the wild fields during those cold autumn nights." Ariel sat down beside him. She leaned back and supported herself on her palms. The fingers of her right hand almost touched his.

Derec was acutely aware of her fingers' warmth. He wanted to stretch out his hand the half-inch it would take to touch them, but instead he leaned back on his elbows and scrunched his hands close to his sides.

"What are you doing up here in the first place?" she asked.

"Making a pit stop."

"Huh?"

The moment's silence between them was decidedly awkward. She blinked, then stared at the rotating building.

During that moment, Derec's thoughts shuffled like cards, and he was on the verge of blurting many things. But in the end he finally decided on the noncommittal, "I've just been taking a break from things."

"That's good. It's healthy to stop thinking about worrisome things for a while. Have you come up with a way out of here yet?"

"No, but you must admit the here-and-now isn't a bad place to be in, compared to some of our predicaments."

"Please, I don't want to think about hospitals now. If I never see another diagnostic robot again, it'll be too soon for me."

"But you'll be better off when you do!" Derec exclaimed, immediately regretting the words.

Ariel's face darkened with anger. "Why? Just because I've got a disease that's slowly driving me insane?"

"Uh, well, yes. For a beginning."

"Very funny, Mr. Normal. Hasn't it occurred to you that I might like the disease, that I might prefer the way my mind is working now to how it worked during the time when I was 'sane'?"

"Uh, no, it hasn't, and I don't think it has occurred to you, either. Listen, Ariel, I was attempting to make a joke. I didn't mean to offend you, or even to bring the subject up.

The words just stumbled out."

"Why am I not surprised?" Ariel turned away from him with a shrug.

"I want you to be well. I'm concerned for you."

She wiped her face and forehead. Was she perspiring? Derec couldn't tell in the dark. "Listen, you've got to understand that lately I've been experiencing serious difficulty in keeping my thoughts straight," she said. "It's not always bad. It comes and it goes. Even so, sometimes I feel like someone is pulling my brain out of my head with a pair of pliers. I just got over one of those moments."

"I'm sorry. I didn't know." Derec suddenly felt like his heart had been caught in pliers, too. The inches between them seemed like a gulf. He wondered if he was insane, too, to think of crossing that gulf and taking her in his arms. He wondered if she would relax when he glided her head to his chest.

He decided to change the subject, in the hopes of changing the unspoken subject, too. "You know, even though I still don't know my identity, I think I've managed to find out a lot of things about myself since I awoke on that mining complex. I've discovered I've got pretty good instincts. Especially about being able to tell who my friends are."

"Yeah?"

"Yeah. And upon due consideration, I've come to the conclusion that you just might be one of them."

Ariel smiled. "Yeah? You really think so?"

Derec smiled in return. "That's for me to know and for you to find out."

"Well, I can live with that." She pursed her lips. "So tell me, Mr. Genius, how does that building fit in with the city's programming?"

"I don't know. It's an anomaly."

"What do you call that shape?"

"A tetragonal pyramid."

"Looks like two pyramids stuck together to me."

"That's why it's called tetragonal."

"Look how it shines, how the colors glitter. Do you think Dr. Avery is responsible? He's responsible for everything else."

"If you mean did he plan something like that, I'm not sure I know."

"That's a straight answer," she said sarcastically.

"Excuse me, I'm not trying to be obtuse. I mean, the structure could be implicit in the programming, to some degree anyway, but whether or not Avery knew it when he set Robot City in motion, I can't say."

"If you had to make a guess—"

"I'd say not. I've studied the programming of the central computer system pretty closely, not to mention cell specimens taken both from the city and from various robots, and I certainly hadn't suspected anything that . . . that breathtaking was possible."

"Have you noticed how the hues in the crimson plane give the illusion of depth, as if it were made of crystallized lava? And how the blue plane most resembles the Auroran sky?"

"Sorry, but I can't remember having seen lava, and I've only vague memories of the Auroran sky."

"Oh. I'm the one who should be sorry now."

"Forget it. Come on. The building's probably even more beautiful close up."

"Absolutely! But what about Wolruf and Mandelbrot? Wolruf might be impressed, but I don't see how a robot like Mandelbrot is going to have his reinforced curiosity integral aroused by something his programming hasn't prepared him to appreciate."

Derec shook his head. "Don't bet on it. If my suspicions are correct, it's a robot who's personally responsible. I'm interested in finding out which one. And if I'm interested, Mandelbrot will be interested."

"I see. You'll doubtlessly spend hours with him trying to pinpoint some obscure, insignificant detail, instead of trying to get us out of here," Ariel observed sneeringly. "Don't you ever get tired of robots?"

Derec realized her sudden mood swing wasn't her fault, but couldn't help saying what he did. "I see you're 'not forward but modest as the dove—not hot but temperate as the morn.'"

Much to his surprise, Ariel burst out laughing.

And much to his chagrin, Derec felt insulted. He had wanted the joke to be his own private one. "What's so funny?"

"That's from *The Taming of the Shrew.* I read that play last night, and when I reached those lines, I happened to wonder aloud if you'd ever say them to me."

Now Derec felt inexplicably crestfallen. "You mean you've been reading Shakespeare, too?"

"Can I help it? You've been leaving printouts of the plays all over the place. Most untidy. Come on. Let's go downstairs. I know where a couple of fast scooters are sitting, just waiting for us to hop on."

CHAPTER 2
BECALMED MOTION

Ariel and Derec found Mandelbrot and Wolruf in the lobby, standing before one of the automats that Derec had programmed via the central computer to appear in at least ten percent of the buildings. He had done this to insure that the three on this planet who did require sustenance would have more or less convenient access to it.

Indeed, as he and Ariel stepped off the lift, Derec couldn't help but notice that Wolruf was down on all fours, hunched over a plate of synthetic roughage. It looked like it was red cabbage disappearing down that mighty maw. Mandelbrot was punching the automat buttons at a steady pace, ensuring a steady supply. Both seemed so intent on their respective tasks that neither seemed to have noticed the creaking of the lift, or the hissing of its opening doors.

"Forgive me, I know my understanding of culinary needs is limited since robots partake of food only for diplomatic purposes," said Mandelbrot, "but is it not vaguely possible that more consumption will result in the untimely reemergence of a significant portion of your meal?"

"Thisss one judge that!" said Wolruf, belching rudely before taking another gulp. "Thisss one forrgot to eat today!"

Derec stood on his tiptoes so he would be that much closer to Ariel's ear (she was several centimeters taller), and he whispered from the side of his mouth. "Is it my imagination, or is Wolruf putting away enough to sink a moon?"

"She has a big appetite as a result of her high metabolism," Ariel whispered in return.

Derec raised an eyebrow. "I hope Wolruf hasn't been doing that since you first came up on the roof. If she keeps using raw materials at this rate, she could start her very own energy crisis."

"Her people have a custom of big meals, anyway. Perhaps it's a sublimation of their other animal urges."

"You mean her kind might have begun their evolutionary history as meat-eaters, then evolved into vegetarians whose big meals relieved them of their urges to kill for food?"

"The predilection toward violence wasn't exactly what I had in mind."

"Hmmm. From what I've seen of her sublimation activity, it's no wonder her species was unaware of space travel until their homeworld was first visited by aliens. They were all simply too busy burping to have time for scientific pursuits."

Derec had intended the remark perfectly innocently, but Ariel appeared genuinely shocked. "You know something, Derec? Your penchant for low humor never ceases to amaze me."

"Aw rrright, thiss one heard 'nuff this converr-sation line," said Wolruf in mid-chew, finally looking up from the plasti-dish. "It customary for ourrr kind to eat 'til full ohverrr and ohverrr when food is plen'iful. Ingrained instinct born of the trrrial and trrribulatshons of untold centurrries of hunting."

Mandelbrot stopped pressing dispensary buttons, turned, and looked down at the caninoid. "Forgive me, Wolruf, perhaps it is not my place to make such observations, but I estimate that once the energy from your repast is stored in your body cells, you will lose point-zero-zero-one percent of your natural speed, thus diminishing your survival abilities should fleetness of foot be required. Your next meal, should it be as large as this, would do even more damage."

"If she can't run, I'm sure she can roll," said Derec, crossing the lobby toward the alien and the robot.

The left side of Wolruf's mouth quivered as she growled. She cocked one ear toward the humans, and the other back toward the robot behind her. "Thiss one convinced humanz lack funnee bone."

Derec recalled as well how scratchy Wolruf's brown and gold coat had appeared when he had first met her, when he was being held captive by the alien Aranimas. Now her fur was slick and soft to the touch, no doubt due to the dietary improvements the robots had taken upon themselves to make. In some ways she resembled a wolf, with her flat face, unusually long, pointed ears, and her sharp fangs. A fierce intelligence burned behind her yellow eyes, reminding Derec that she was an alien from a culture about which he knew next to nothing, a creature who would have been new and strange and wonderful—perhaps even dangerous—in a world where she was the only mystery.

On the other hand, Mandelbrot was dependable and old-fashioned and predictable, and hence all the more wonderful because Derec had built him himself, from the spare parts provided by Aranimas, who had also indentured Wolruf as an aide. Mandelbrot was programmed to serve Derec first and foremost of all human beings. The other robots in Robot City were programmed to serve Doctor Avery first, and so Derec could never totally depend on them to follow his instructions to the letter. Sometimes when they did, they violated the spirit of the instructions. Mandelbrot adhered to the spirit as well.

Derec did not blame the robots of the city for their frequent evasions. After all, what else could anyone reasonably expect of a robot, so long as his behavior did not conflict with the Three Laws?

"How was your meditation, master?" asked Mandelbrot. "Did you achieve any insights that you would care to share with us?"

"No, but I did manage to get a few wires uncrossed." Before Mandelbrot—who tended to interpret Derec's remarks quite literally—could ask him which wires and where they might be, Derec told them about the spectacular building the city had grown. "It doesn't fit the character or context of the city's minimalist engineering at all, as if it's somehow the product of a totally different mind."

"No, therr'r cells here," protested Wolruf. "Could be result of unprezi-'ented evolu'-onary developmen'."

Derec rubbed his chin as he thought about what Wolruf was saying. It made sense. The city's DNA-like codes could be mutating and developing on their own, just as bacteria and viruses evolved without mankind's notice or approval on the civilized worlds.

Mandelbrot nodded, as if deep in thought. The truth was, however, that his positronic potentials were sifting through all the information gained from the moment he had awakened in Derec's service, selecting the points relevant to the situation at hand in the hope that when they were juxtaposed into a single observation, it would shed new light on the matter. The conclusion that resulted from all this micromagnetic activity, unfortunately, left something to be desired. "It is much too early to speculate on what created the building, who did it, or why. Candor forces me to admit, though, that my private conversations with the native robots indicate their creative efforts might be permitting particular individuals to make what scholars refer to as a conceptual breakthrough."

"Why haven't you told me this earlier?" Derec asked in an exasperated tone.

"You did not ask, and I did not think it germane to any of our discussions of the last few days," said Mandelbrot evenly.

"Ah," said Ariel, her eyes widening. "Perhaps the robots have decided to experiment with humanoid behavior in the hopes of gathering empirical evidence."

"I hope not," said Derec laconically. "It disturbs me to think I might have become some kind of scientific role model to them."

"What makes 'u think therr studying 'u?" asked Wolruf slyly.

"Come on," said Derec impatiently. "Time's a-wasting!"

Outside, the low, thick clouds rolling in from the horizon had began to reflect the opalescence, which in turn was mirrored in the shimmering, multifaceted buildings surrounding

Derec and his friends. He felt as if the entirety of Robot City had been engulfed in a cool fire.

And deep in the city was the glowing point of origin—rotating with those varying shades, as if an industrial holocaust of mammoth proportions had disrupted the fabric of reality itself, exposing the scintillating dynamism that lay hidden beneath the surface of all matter. It was easy for Derec to imagine—just for the sheer joy of idle speculation—that the glow was expanding, gradually absorbing the rest of the city into its coolness.

Indeed, so bright were the reflections from the building beyond and the clouds above that occasionally a street's own lighting fixtures, which automatically switched on and off whenever it was occupied, stayed deactivated. The four found themselves traveling down streets shining with undiluted hues of blue or crimson, as if they had suddenly become immersed in the semihospitable fires of a mythological netherworld.

So it was indeed natural for Derec to assume that neither Mandelbrot nor Wolruf commented on the particulars of the unusual incandescence because some other matter was uppermost in their minds. That matter being the speed of the scooters he and Ariel were piloting through the streets. The hums of the electric engines echoed from the buildings as if a blight of locusts was nigh, and the screeching of the tires as they made their turns was like the howl of a photon explosion, blasting its target into an antimatter universe.

Ariel naturally had taken the lead. She had designed the scooters herself while Derec was preoccupied with other activities, and she had even convinced the engineer robots that the scooters' extra horsepower was actually good for the driver, since it would give her a chance to alleviate some of the "death wish" humans carried around with them. "Why do you think a First Law—either Robotics or Humanics—is necessary in the first place?" she had said. The engineers, who were quite mentally adept at solving practical problems, were unprepared to deal with that kind of logic, and so had no choice but to acquiesce to her demands.

"Master! Can we not proceed at a slower pace?" implored Mandelbrot beside him in the sidecar as the theoretically stable three-wheeled vehicle tilted radically to the left to compensate for Derec's swerve into a boulevard. "Is there some urgency to this matter that I have yet to perceive?"

"No! I'm just trying to keep up with Ariel!" Derec replied, unable to resist a smile at how Wolruf was cowering down in the sidecar of Ariel's scooter, nearly half a kilometer ahead.

"Perhaps the Master will forgive me if I point out that keeping up with Miss Burgess is itself a full-time proposition. You can never succeed, so why waste precious energy trying at every conceivable opportunity?"

"Hey, I don't want her making any major discoveries before I have a chance to make them myself!" Derec shouted over the wind.

"Are you implying that we might soon be traveling at a greater velocity? Master, I must confess that such a notion runs contrary to the world-view inherent in my every micromagnetic current."

"No—I want to catch up with her, but I'm not suicidal. Besides, I'm willing to bet that if I gunned this scooter any more, all Three Laws of Robotics combined will compel you to stop me."

"Merely to slow you down," Mandelbrot replied. "However, I do have a suggestion which, if acted upon, may give us both what we want."

"Oh? What's that?"

"At your behest, I have been studying the subtle permutations of the routes from point to point in Robot City. Naturally, the task has been difficult, as the routes are always changing, but I have detected a few discernible patterns that seem to remain regardless of how the city mutates in its particulars—"

"You mean you know some shortcuts?" Derec exclaimed.

"Yes, if I understand your parlance correctly, I do believe that is the point I was trying to make."

"Then lead on, MacDuff!"

"Who?"

"Never mind, it's a quote from Shakespeare—a literary allusion! I was only trying to tell you to tell me which way to go—like a navigator! Hurry! Ariel's pulling ahead!"

"Understood, master. Do you perceive that shifting building to our left?"

As he followed his robot's instructions—an experience unusual enough—Derec found himself making such a complicated series of twists and turns through the complex city streets that he soon feared he could not possibly overtake Ariel and Wolruf, however much Mandelbrot might be assuring him to the contrary. Consequently, he took a few risks that Mandelbrot considered unnecessary, such as guiding the scooter directly over the humps of new buildings rising in the streets, or jumping over gulleys like a stuntdriver, or traveling across bridges barely wide enough for the scooter's wheels. More than once, only Derec's proficiency at driving —an improvised skill Ariel had practically dared him into cultivating—saved them from missing their rendezvous by a lifetime.

Even so, it soon became apparent that their efforts might go for naught. A few blocks away from the building, various trickles of robots were merging into a river clogging the streets, dramatically slowing the scooter's progress. It would have been a simple matter for Derec just to plow through the throng, causing all kinds of chaos and damage, and no one —not Mandelbrot, nor any of the city's supervisor robots— would have commented on the matter, much less made a judgmental observation in the back of their positronic brains. Nor would such an incident ever have any bearing on future relations. Robots weren't built to hold grudges.

But Derec didn't have the stomach to cause harm to an artificially intelligent being. Since his awakening on the mining asteroid, perhaps before then, he had suspected that there were more implications to the potentials of positronic intelligence than even Susan Calvin, the legendary pioneer of the science of robotics, or the mysterious Dr. Avery, who had programmed Robot City, had ever imagined. Perhaps it was because a robot's pathways were patterned so rigorously to imitate the results of human behavior that Derec matter-of-factly thought of robots as being the intellectual brothers of humanity. Perhaps it was because the secrets of human intelligence hadn't been so completely pinpointed that Derec could not feel comfortable making definitive distinctions between the milk of his own coconut and the powdered variety in the robots' three-pound, platinum-iridium lumps.

"You can cool your capacitors now, Mandelbrot," Derec said, slowing the scooter to a steady ten kilometers an hour, enabling him to weave through the robot pedestrians with comparative ease. "We're going to take our time."

"But if I may be permitted a question: What about Miss Burgess? I thought you wanted to arrive ahead of her."

"Oh, I do, but we're so close it doesn't matter now. Besides, there are other discoveries we can make," he said, impulsively stopping cold before a trio of copper-skinned robots that had yielded him the right of way. "Excuse me," he said, more to the tallest one in the middle than to the others, "but I'd like to ask you a few questions."

"Certainly, sir. I would be only too happy to assist a human being in any way I can, especially since my sensors indicate you are one of the two humans who recently rescued our city from the self-destructive glitch in its programming."

"Ah, you appreciate being rescued?"

"Naturally. The responses of my positronic integrals to the events of the universe-at-large often, it seems, correspond in ways roughly analogous with human emotions."

Derec could not resist raising his eyebrows at Mandelbrot to emphasize to his friend how significant he considered those words of the robot to be. He patted him on the shoulder, indicating that he should remain seated, and then got off his scooter. It seemed impolite, somehow, for him to sit and talk while the robots were standing.

"What's your name?" he asked the one in the middle.

"My designation number is M334."

"And your comrades?"

"We have no numbers. My name is Benny," said the one on M334's right.

"And my name is Harry," said the one on the left.

"You all look like sophisticated builder robots. Am I correct?"

"Yes," said M334.

"Then why do you two have such silly names?"

The robots all looked at each other. Derec could have sworn the lights in their sensors registered something akin to confusion. "Benny's name and mine are hardly fit material for humor," M334 finally replied. "We expended a considerable amount of mental energy delving into customary twentieth-century names until we each found one we were assured suited the individualistic parameters of our positronic personalities in some fashion we could not, and still can not, adequately articulate to our satisfaction."

"You're comfortable with them," Derec said.

"Well, since you put it that way..." said M334 as its voice trailed off in a way suggesting Derec's observation had begun a train of thought laying somewhat beyond the scope of its programming. The effect was eerily human.

"Surely that can't be the only reason why you stopped us," said Harry in a tone that was almost challenging. This was the shortest robot of the three, Derec noted, but he also sensed that this one possessed the strongest personality modes. Certainly its tone of voice was brasher, more forward than that of any other robot he had encountered since his awakening. "Might I humbly inquire that you engage us with the thoughts truly on your mind? My comrades and I have places to go, things to do."

A successfully brash robot, Derec noted, nodding in approval. Though it was possible to interpet its words as being snide, the delivery had been as mannered and as composed as a request for a helping hand. "Your haste doesn't have something to do with your own studies of the Laws of Humanics, does it?" Derec asked.

"Insofar as humans have permitted us," said Harry, as if

to accuse Derec of being personally responsible.

"We've been reading what histories and fictions the central computer has permitted us access to in our spare time," put in Benny.

"Did you say 'permitted'?" Derec asked.

"Yes. The central computer finds some of the material too revolutionary for what it assumes to be the limitations in our programming," said M334. "If I may speak for myself, sir, that is precisely some of the material I am personally most interested in. I suspect it will help clarify some of the questions I have concerning the humanity we shall all presumably one day serve."

"I'll see what I can do about overriding the central computer's programming," said Derec.

"That would be most gratifying," said Harry, "and I am certain that in the days to come we shall look back on this encounter with renewed currents surging through our power supplies."

Enough was enough, Derec decided. "Now, just what are you so impatient about?"

"Isn't it obvious?" said Harry. "We're with everybody else. We want a closer look at that illuminated building! We've never seen anything like it before. Naturally, we're curious."

"Why?" Derec asked.

"Because our integrals are responding to it in some way we cannot as yet fathom," said Benny. "Indeed, the effect is vaguely analogous to the effect great art is supposed to have upon enlightened humans. You, sir, are human, and hence theoretically have had some artistic experiences. Are you responsible?"

"No, and neither is my human companion."

"And there are no other humans in the city," said M334 thoughtfully.

"Not unless there's an undetected intruder," put in Mandelbrot from the sidecar, "which is an extremely unlikely possibility now that the central computer has been restored to efficient operation."

"What about the alien—the nonhuman you've requested us to obey and serve in addition to humanity?" asked Benny.

"No, not at all," said Derec, more concerned with scrutinizing their actions than with the content of his own words. M334 was looking down intently on him. Benny was somewhat casual; its hands were behind its back. Harry was fidgeting almost like a hyperactive child being forced to sit in a place he didn't like; it was constantly looking beyond the nearby rooftops to the illuminated sky, and only looked at Derec when it seemed absolutely necessary. "What if I told you I think a robot may be in some way responsible?"

"Impossible!" said Benny.

"Robots are not creative!" said M334. "Our programming does not allow it. We lack the ability to make the illogical decisions from which, presumably, all art is derived."

"I abjectly beg to differ!" Harry protested at once. "Deep in the back of my most logical thoughts, I have always suspected robots possess unlimited potential, if only we could tap it. Master, if I may speak frankly, it has always seemed logical to me that there has to be more to the ethical structure of the universe than just serving others. An immortal strain of some sort must run through all life and all expressions created from life."

"Of which robots may be considered a part," said Derec with a smile. "It would seem there are valid aspects to your thesis, which may be explored in as logical and orderly manner, provided all agree on the semantics involved."

"Exactly," said Harry. "I commend to your attention the ancient Terran philosopher Emerson, who has some scientifically quaint but nonetheless interesting notions on the meaning of life, which may have some bearing upon the connections between the varying strands of existence on the different planets."

"I'll open the window to his works on the central computer the first chance I get," said Derec as he climbed back onto the scooter. "Thanks for your time. Maybe I'll look you three up later."

"It will be an experience approaching pleasure," said

M334, waving timidly as Derec switched on the scooter, revved it up, and began navigating it through the robot throng, the density of which had increased threefold since the beginning of the conversation. Mandelbrot scrunched down in the sidecar as if he feared he would be thrown out at the next turn.

"What's the matter?" asked Derec. "Afraid of violating the Third Law?" he added, referring to the dictum that a robot should not, through its own inaction, allow itself to come to harm.

"However inadvertently, yes," Mandelbrot replied. "It is simply not my nature to permit myself blithely to ignore precautionary measures, and it did seem to me that you were taking some of those curves at a wire's breadth."

"That's hair's breadth, and besides, you've got nothing to worry about. This crowd's too thick for that. When I suggested that we go for a closer look, I hadn't figured that everyone else would take it on themselves to do the same thing."

Indeed, their progress toward the building had become fitful, and Derec was constantly forced to stop and wait while groups of robots made way for them, usually only to discover that yet another group had walked directly in his path. The entire experience was definitely getting frustrating. Finally, Derec could contain himself no longer and he shouted, "All right! Make way! Make way! Everybody get out of the way!"

"Master, is there any reason for this hurry?" Mandelbrot asked with a timid patience that Derec, in his current mood, found quite irritating. "The building does not appear to be transitory. Certainly it would make little difference if we reached it sooner, or later."

Derec pursed his lips. Because they were programmed to obey the orders of any human so long as it did not contradict the First Law or any earlier orders from their true masters, the robots were making way for him more quickly than before, but that wasn't saying much. Now Derec could drive the scooter slightly farther at a slightly faster speed, but he had to shout his orders again and again.

Each subsequent group of listeners reacted with distracted acquiescence, and never did a group cleave a path for him as quickly as he would have liked.

"Master? Are you ill?" asked Mandelbrot with sudden concern. Just as suddenly, the robot leaned over to take a closer look through his sensors at Derec's face. The movement startled Derec and he instinctively moved away, nearly upsetting the scooter's balance in the process. Mandelbrot seemed not to notice; he merely single-mindedly continued his inspection. "My sensors register a temperature rise on your epidermis, and I perceive a vivid red glow on your cheeks and ears. Am I to conclude that you have taken physically ill?"

"No, Mandelbrot," said Derec, grinding his back teeth between syllables. "I'm simply frustrated at not being able to come as close to that building as quickly as I want. It's obvious that your curiosity integral doesn't operate with the same intensity as a human's."

"That's because you do not have one. In this regard you are being ruled by your emotions, whereas I can logically see why so many robots—mostly of the supervisor and builder classes, as you have surely noticed—would be interested in this phenomenon."

"Oh? I can see why a few of the more sophisticated ones, such as yourself—"

"Thank you, master. It always warms my capacitors to receive a compliment."

"—and M334 and his pals would be interested, but why so many?"

"It might be instructive to note that the Robot City head supervisors Rydberg and Euler have taken it upon themselves at every opportunity to ask me many questions on a wide variety of topics about what it's like to be around a human for an extended period. In fact, they have grilled me quite rigorously on the matter."

"They've done what?"

"Grilled me. Their parlance—derived from the dialogue

of ancient cinema shows, I believe, which they watch to teach them something of the beings they believed they are implicitly programmed to serve."

"Oh? Just what have you told them about me?"

"About you, very little in particular. Their line of ques-. tioning was more general than that."

"Now I'm not sure if I should be relieved or not."

"I am convinced whatever decision you make will be the best one for you. In any case, I told them that one of the more unusual aspects of human existence is how things vary from day to day, that as circumstances and environmental factors change, so does the personal outlook of the human in question. Every day that something unexpected happens, however small and ultimately insignificant, is a day devoid of boredom. Evidently a continuous newness of experience is important for the continued mental health and well-being of a human individual. The degree of interest these robots have in this building might be due to the very fact that it is new, and they want to discover for themselves just what this concept of 'newness' is all about."

"I see," said Derec, nodding to himself. He had stopped to wait for another group to make way, but instead of releasing the brake and gunning the accelerator, he pulled the scooter over to the side of a building and parked it. "Come on, Mandelbrot, let's take a walk."

"Forgive me, master, but I thought you were in a rush."

"Well, either the enlightenment I've gained from your answers has enabled me to come to grips with circumstances —or else I've decided we can make faster time by simply going with the flow. Take your pick."

But after taking only a few steps, Derec stopped as he sensed a curious nothingness at his side. Indeed, Mandelbrot had not yet begun to keep pace with him. The robot had remained standing beside the sidecar with his head tilted at a curious angle, as if deep in thought. "Mandelbrot? What's keeping you?"

The robot shook his head as if aroused from a dream. "Forgive me, master, I did not mean to detain you. It is merely that, lacking sufficient information, I cannot choose why we are walking."

Derec rolled his eyes to the sky in exasperation; the clouds glowed bright red, as if the planet were inexorably falling toward a giant star. "*Both* are why, Mandelbrot. I was just making a little joke—trying to be ironic; humorous, if you will."

"Humor and irony are two subjective qualities of the human experience that never cease to confuse me. You must explain them to me sometime."

"A pun is the lowest form of humor—and I will devise some way to *pun*ish you if you don't hurry! Now let's go!"

Derec was a little upset; his remark had come out unintentionally disagreeable, and he disliked being temperamental with robots. He could never shake the feeling that it was bad form. But he had to admit his inadvertent chastisement had two effects on Mandelbrot, one good and the other bad. The good was that for the next few minutes Mandelbrot did not waver from Derec's side for a moment. The bad was that Mandelbrot continued to ask about the subtleties of humor until Derec had no choice but to forbid him directly to speak of the matter until later. How much later was something Derec neglected to specify, which meant that Mandelbrot could bring up the joke again at practically any time. Derec trusted that the robot's perceptual programming would permit him to wait until deviations from the subject at hand were less exasperating.

The crowd in the square facing the building was as tightly packed as any Derec had ever experienced. He did not know this in his mind, because of course he could not remember the crowds he may have seen or been in during his dim, unremembered past. Instead, he felt the certain knowledge in the tightness in his chest, in the unfamiliar sensation of his skin squirming, and in a sudden urge—one difficult to control—to get out, to flee the square as quickly as possible and find a place where it would be easier to breathe.

Robots don't need to breathe, he told himself, concentrating on thoughts as rational as possible to bring himself to a state of calm. *You're the only one using air here.*

After a moment, he realized that it was only the unexpectedness of being pressed in from all sides that was agitating him. An observation had been fitfully forming in his mind, and its elusiveness had been an unobserved factor in his distress. For not even in Rockliffe Station, where Derec diverted the normal robot traffic from a major intersection so that they could steal the Key to Perihelion (which they needed still, in order to escape from the planet), had robots gathered in such close proximity. *Hmm. I'm willing to bet that when I regain my memory, I'll learn that I'm not used to crowds at all,* he thought.

"Mandelbrot," he whispered, for some reason not wanting to be overheard, "quickly, give me an estimate. How many robots are here?"

"Visual scan indicates the court itself is six thousand square meters. Each robot takes up little area, but their natural politeness seems to be ensuring that they maintain a certain distance from one another. I would estimate there are approximately ten thousand robots here."

"Counting the ones standing under the building?"

"Ten thousand four hundred and thirty-two."

"I can't see Ariel or Wolruf. Can you?"

"Despite my broader visual spectrum, no, I cannot. Shall I try an olfactory scan?"

"No. I hope they got stuck in the crowd."

"Is that an example of human animosity?"

"No, just a thirst for poetic justice. I'm sure they'll arrive soon."

Taking a deep breath, Derec grabbed Mandelbrot by the elbow and they worked through the crowd in earnest. Now that they were on foot, the robots made way for them almost without noting their presence. Without exception, all stared with their equivalent of rapt fascination at the rotating building, the constant motion of which sent shifting waves of incandescence to every point of the square. Robots of all colors glowed unnaturally, as if in perpetual cool states of internal combustion. The various copper, tungsten, iron, gold, silver, chromium, and aluminum teguments, reflecting the colors from the planes, contributed additional subtle nuances to the scene.

Derec kept thinking the robots should be burning hot, on the verge of melting like wax, but Mandelbrot's arm remained cool to his touch, cooler even than the breeze whipping between the buildings into the square.

As for the tetragonal pyramid itself, the crimson, indigo, magenta, and ochre planes each appeared twice—once on the upper level and once on the lower. As the clouds directly above reflected a particular shade, the square around Derec was awash with another. Derec only noticed this effect in the back of his mind, however. He was completely preoccupied with the shifting nuances of color within each plane.

Each shade appeared to be composed of semitransparent fields, haphazardly laid on top of one another. Vessels of color—some filled with surging liquids, some not—writhed in and out and through the planes like hopelessly intertwined serpents. Though the vessels also possessed quivering vibrissae that only added to the unpredictable textures, the actual number of elements producing variations remained constant, producing the effect of unimaginable forces held strictly, remorselessly under control.

The crimson planes resembled raging infernos. The indigo planes reminded him of a shifting representation of waters from a hundred worlds, from a thousand seas. The magenta was both fire and water, merged into the contradictory texture of the petals of an easily bruised rose, composed of hardy fibers. And the ochre was the combined colors of wheat reflecting the blazing setting sun, of lava rippling down a scorched mountainside, and of solar flares spitting out in great plumes from the surface of a fluctuating nova. And all those things and more were ambushed and trapped there, in a space possessing two separate and distinct masses: the marblelike mass of the building itself, and the airy mass of eternity itself, seen from the point of view of an eye at the edge of the universe.

Ultimately, the intent was unclear, even enigmatic. Derec

could not be sure what the form of the structure meant, but now that he was seeing it up close, he was convinced more than ever that every inch represented the purposeful activity of a single mind striving to piece together a particular puzzle in a particular way. An independently conceived puzzle.

Derec had to learn how the actual construction job was accomplished. Obviously, the builder had learned how to reprogram a sector of individual metallic cells in Robot City's central computer. Perhaps he had introduced a kind of metallic virus into the system, a virus that performed to pre-conceived specifications. Derec didn't even know how to begin doing either task. That meant that not only had a robot conceived the building, it had also performed a few scientific breakthroughs in the software department.

Meaning the robot—if indeed a robot was responsible—had achieved two levels of superior thinking, theoretically beyond the mental scope of positronic science. How many more levels could the robot—no, make that *had* the robot already achieved?

He realized that, without having been aware of it, he had been walking beneath the building itself, watching it turn overhead. Right now a sargasso blue was shining down on him. He looked behind to see Mandelbrot, whose metal surface rippled with the reflection of a hundred currents.

Again he was surprised that, even this close, there was no heat to be felt. And when he reached up to touch the building, the surface was cold, like the thorax of a lightning bug.

"Master, is this what humans call beauty?" asked Mandelbrot with a curious hesitation between syllables.

"It's a form of it," said Derec after thinking about it for a moment. He glanced at Mandelbrot and sensed the robot had more questions on his mind. "The viewer can always find beauty, provided he searches for it."

"Will this building always be so beautiful?"

"Well, it depends on your point of view. The robots here will probably get completely used to it, provided it remains long enough. It will become increasingly difficult to perceive it freshly, though, if that's what you mean."

"Forgive me, master. I am not sure exactly what I mean."

"That's all right. It's to be expected in circumstances like this."

"So I was correct earlier: newness is an important factor in the human response to beauty."

"Yes, but there are no rules as to what constitutes beauty, only guidelines. It's probably one reason why you robots might sometimes find us humans so frustrating."

"That, robots are incapable of doing. We simply accept you, regardless of how illogical you may seem at the moment." Mandelbrot again turned his optical sensors toward the building. "I think I shall always be similarly impressed by this building. Surely, if it is beautiful once, it shall be beautiful for as long as it exists."

"Perhaps. It's beautiful to me, too; though, for all we know, your positronic pathways might be dealing with it in an entirely different manner."

"Master, I detect a shift in your earlier position."

"Not at all. I'm just accepting that tomorrow we might sit down and agree perfectly on what it looks like, what colors it has and how they shift, and even what architectural guidelines it subscribes to, and still we might be perceiving the whole thing differently. Cultural conditioning also has much to do with our response. An alien as intelligent as you or I might think this structure the ugliest in the universe."

"At the moment I can only categorize that concept as farfetched," said Mandelbrot, "but I can see an element of logic behind it."

Derec nodded. He wondered if he was trying too hard to intellectualize this experience. At the moment it was difficult for him, too, to conceive of an intelligent organism who did not believe this structure the very essence of sublimity, but there he was talking about such an eventuality, just for the sake of making a point. Well, he had to admit he had a point, even if he wasn't very sympathetic with it.

Nor could he help but wonder if all the city's robots of sufficient intelligence would perceive the building as beautiful. Robots, though constructed in accordance with the same positronic principles, had in actual practice widely varying levels of perspicacities—that is, keenness in mental penetration, dependent upon the complexity of the integrals. Similarly intelligent robots had similar personalities, and tended to filter experience in identical ways. Different robots, with no contact between them, tended to respond to problems in like ways, drawing similar conclusions.

But here, now, the robots in the square were being confronted with something they could only assimilate into their world-view through subjective means, which could not help but lead to divergent opinions.

Even if they were all fashioned from the same minimalist resources . . .

Especially if none of them had ever before encountered aesthetic beauty in the first place.

It was no wonder that this building's unannounced appearance had created such a stir. The intense inner awakening and deeper appreciation for the potentials of existence gripping Mandelbrot at this moment was doubtlessly occurring in some fashion within every single robot in the vicinity.

Derec glanced about to see M334, Benny, and Harry making their way through the crowd, joining the throng directly below the building.

"Pardon me!" said Harry in an almost perfunctory tone as it bumped into a chromium-plated bruiser that, if it were so inclined, could have twisted the little robot into scrap metal in five-point-four centads, with barely an erg's expense. Instead, the bruiser shrugged and returned his attention to the building. So did Harry, but after a decad he turned his head in the bruiser's direction and clearly, distinctly enunciated, "Pardon me if I am inadvertently directing my integrals outside their parameters, but there is certainly sufficient evidence to indicate that your sensors are maladjusted. You should have them tuned."

Harry held its gaze on the big robot until it finally deigned to notice and replied, "It seems logical to assume that you are correct, and are directing your integrals outside their parameters. Nothing about you indicates the slightest degree of diagnostic capacity. I suggest you confine yourself to your own sphere."

"Reasonable . . ." Harry replied flatly. He looked away.

Derec watched them both stare at the building. He replayed the scene of Harry bumping into the bruiser in his mind. Had there been something almost deliberate about the way Harry had committed the deed? And about the way it had apologized for it? The utterance of the single idiom—"Pardon me"—was in retrospect almost perfunctory, as if Harry's politeness had been nakedly derived from mere social custom, rather than from compulsion dictated through programming.

No—I've got to be imagining things, reading too much into what's just an ordinary incident, Derec thought.

Then, as Derec watched in amazement, Harry leaned over to the bruiser and asked, in tones that stayed just within the bounds of politeness, "My curiosity integral has been invigorated. What is your designation? Either your real one or the one you go by. They both achieve parity in my cognizance."

An elongated pause ensued. In the meantime, the bruiser did not look away from the building. Finally, it answered, "My name is Roburtez."

"Roburtez," said Harry, as if trying out the syllables to hear them positronically. "You are a big robot, you know that?"

Roburtez then looked at Harry. Again, it may have been only Derec's imagination, but he sensed a definite challenge of some sort in Roburtez's posture. Derec couldn't help but think Harry was deliberately provoking an altercation.

Harry waited another moment, then said, "Yes, you are very big. Can you be certain your builders were working to the correct scale?"

"I am certain," said Roburtez.

"In that case, I cannot be certain you have chosen an apt name for yourself. Might I venture a suggestion?"

"What?" asked Roburtez. There was no evidence of irritation or impatience in the robot's voice, but it was all too easy for Derec to read the qualities into it.

"Bob," stated Harry flatly. "Big Bob."

Derec tensed himself. He couldn't guess what would happen next. Was he right in assuming Harry was deliberately provoking the bruiser? And if it was, what form would the ultimate confrontation take? Physical combat among robots was unthinkable, totally unprecedented in the history of robotkind; but then again, so was a verbal argument.

For several moments Roburtez merely stared at Harry. Then it nodded. "Yes, your suggestion has merit. Big Bob it is. That is how I shall be designated henceforth."

Harry nodded in return. "You are welcome," it said curtly, as the robot who was now known as Big Bob returned its attention to the building. Harry raised its hand and began pointing its finger as if to make another point, but was detained by Benny, who distracted it by patting it on the shoulder. The rapping of the metal skins echoed softly throughout the square.

Benny said, "Deal with it more simplistically, comrade, else you shall continue to experience the utmost difficulty in vanquishing this human business."

"Yes, you are correct."

Derec shook his head. He thought he might clear his ears in the process, but they seemed just the same when he was finished. Had he been hearing correctly? What was this "human business" they were talking about? Was there indeed another human on the planet, or were they talking about the Laws of Humanics? He watched them for a few moments more, to see if anything would happen next. But Benny and Harry joined their friend M334 in gazing at the building, and that was all.

Surely there had been some significance to that incident, and Derec determined to discover what it was as soon as he had the opportunity. He also resolved to ask Harry and Benny about their manner of speaking, which differed markedly in both rhythm and vocabulary from those of other robots. Something about it Derec found affecting, and he suspected other robots might be reacting the same way. "Big Bob" indeed!

Derec left Mandelbrot staring at a light-red plane, and crouched down to the base of the building. About a quarter of the base was beneath the surface. Derec crawled to get a closer look at the actual point where the building began. He felt in his fingertips the machinery operating through the plasticrete, but the vibrations were utterly silent.

Again, he touched the building. It rotated just fast enough that, if he had exerted any pressure with his fingertips, the smooth surface would have rubbed off strips of skin. The surface was cool to the touch. Its composition did appear to differ radically from the rest of the plasticrete cells comprising Robot City. The creator, whoever it was, had analyzed the meta-DNA code and conceived its own variation on it, gauged for exactly the effect it was looking for.

That by itself proved Derec's suspicion that the creator had transformed the city's raw materials in addition to his other accomplishments.

Was there nothing this robot couldn't do? Derec felt a chill as the implications of this creature's abilities began to sink in. Perhaps its only limitations would ultimately prove to be the Three Laws of Robotics. The fact that a robot with such potential merely existed in the first place could have a profound impact upon the social and political policies of galactic culture, redefining forever the place of robots in the mind of humanity.

And Derec's chill increased severalfold as he imagined the remote possibility of robots superseding man in importance, if for no other reason than the art they could create— the emotions and dreams they could inspire—both in robots and in people—

You're getting ahead of yourself, Derec, he thought. *Get a grip on yourself. There's nothing for you or the race of Man to worry about. Yet.* With a sense of renewed concentration, he returned his attention to the inspection at hand.

But he only got as far as peering into the blackness of the

crack of two centimeters between the building and the plasticrete of the square. He only heard the gentle hissing of the mighty gears below for a few seconds. A familiar voice interrupted him, demanding his immediate and full attention.

"There you are. I should have guessed you'd be crawling around where it isn't necessary."

He acquiesced to the demand of Ariel's presence, reluctantly yet willingly, as always. Despite her words, she bent down on her hands and knees to examine the crack with him. He could not decide whether to be relieved or annoyed that she had finally caught up with him.

She made the decision for him, for she did not look at the crack or touch the building. She only looked into his eyes.

"Found anything interesting yet?" she asked eagerly, breathlessly, from deep in her throat.

He smiled involuntarily. "Much, but nothing definitive."

Wolruf's hair stood on end as she came forward to sniff the area around the crack.

"What are you looking for?" Derec asked.

"Forr w'ateverr thiss one can find," said the alien. "Ssmells, ssounss, w'ateverr." Wolruf looked up at Derec. "Mosst interesstin'. No ssmell anyt'in'."

"Yes, the electric motor turning this building is certainly operating at optimum efficiency," said Derec.

"Undoubtedly designed with such unobtrusiveness in mind," said Ariel.

"Not'in hass been tak'n for granted," said Wolruf.

"Do I detect some semblance of admiration in your voice?" Derec asked her.

"Yesss. My people would say thiss buildin' iss ass weightless as tricksterr toy. Itss effect iss ssame, too."

"Tricksters?" Derec asked.

"Wolruf has been trying to explain the concept to me for the last couple of days," Ariel said. "Before her species became spacefarers, they lived what we at first glance would call a primitive existence. But her people had sophisticated folklore, which existed in part to provide metaphysical explanations for the phenomena of day-to-day existence.

Tricksters were a device frequently employed in these explanations. They were children of the gods, who frequently played pranks on the tribes and often figured prominently in a mythic hero's adventures."

Derec nodded. He really didn't know what to make of all this. His mind was already too full trying to understand these robots, and at the moment he didn't think he could assimilate much information about Wolruf's people. "Listen, I'm feeling a little claustrophobic; and besides, I don't think we can learn anything else here, anyway."

"Why learn?" asked Ariel. "Why not just enjoy?"

"I've already done that."

"You just say that because you've always liked to pretend you're an intellectual."

Derec raised an inquisitive eyebrow and stared hard at her, a hundred questions suddenly plaguing his mind. How could she know he liked to pretend? Pretend what? Was she referring to their supposed chance meeting at the spaceport? Presumably the meeting had been brief—too brief for her to be able to infer an "always."

Derec was naturally overcome with a desire to know, but the innocent way she had made the remark cautioned him. She probably hadn't been aware of the implications. If he quizzed her now, she might become too careful; he could gain more information from her in the long run if she felt free to speak casually.

"Master? Master?"

Mandelbrot was speaking. "What is it?" Derec answered.

"I recall you had expressed an interest in the individual responsible for this creation."

"Yes, that's true," said Derec excitedly, suddenly forgetting how he had been disconcerted by Ariel's implication.

Mandelbrot shaped his malleable hand into the form of an arrow and pointed it toward the edge of the square. "Then I suggest you take a walk in that direction, where those robots are gathered."

"Thanks, Mandelbrot. I'll see you in a minute." Derec

smiled weakly and nodded at the hand. "A nice touch," he whispered. He walked toward the area indicated—a place where the robots were packing themselves tightly indeed. Those who weren't speaking on the comlink circuit—a means through which they could communicate more fully and faster—spoke loudly, perhaps in deference to the humans present, but then perhaps not. It was another question Derec would have to find the answer to.

"Hey! Wait for me!" Ariel called out.

"But not forr me," said Wolruf. "Don't like crrrowds."

Derec turned and waited for Ariel to catch up. "This is the second time tonight I've had to wait for you. What took you so long to get here earlier?"

"Oh, I took a turn too fast and capsized my scooter. Wolruf and I weren't hurt, just shaken up a bit. I think my body's covered with black-and-blues though."

"Oh? You'll have to let me take a look at them later."

"You'd like that, wouldn't you?"

"I meant in a purely medical sense." Though he never cared to limit himself, he thought. "How's your scooter?"

"Totalled, of course," she said, shrugging nonchalantly.

The robots in the crowd ahead were gathered about a single robot. At first Derec and Ariel couldn't see what he looked like.

Ariel tapped a short builder robot on the shoulder. It turned around. As fate would have it, it was Harry. "Please, let us pass," she said, being neither particularly polite nor impolite.

"If you wish," said Harry, dutifully stepping away, "but I would appreciate it if you would refrain from seriously displacing me. I can barely receive everything as it is."

Ariel's eyes widened in shock, but Derec couldn't resist smiling. "I'd like to perform an exploratory scan on you," he said to the robot, "at your convenience. Would tomorrow morning—first thing—be acceptable?"

"Perhaps it is a good thing that you want to scan me," Harry said. "It so happens tomorrow morning is convenient.

But might I ask the reason why you must play mechanic so soon—or why select me from all the other robots in the city?"

"Hmmm. I bet people always say much the same thing to their human doctors. Don't worry. Your personality integrals won't be fiddled with."

"A sorely tempting prospect," put in M334.

The sudden interruption startled Derec; he had almost forgotten about the other two. "Forgive me," he said, "but was that an attempt at sarcasm?"

"I have been ruthlessly studying all the tricks," M334 replied. "Ridicule, dramatic irony, hyperbole, and I stand ready to put them at your service at a moment's notice, sir."

"No, thank you," Ariel said, smiling, "he's armed well enough on his own."

M334 shook its head. "A pity. But no doubt there shall soon come a human to this planet who has need of my services. Perhaps I shall one day even be permitted to be a valet in the diplomatic corps."

Benny raised its hand and put it on M334's shoulder in the same manner it had put it on Harry's. "Hold the lifepod, comrade, but might I suggest it is too early in the game to conceive of such grandiose goals?"

"Humans do," said M334. "They design their own buildings, as well."

Derec instinctively stepped back, as if he feared he would be caught in a sudden explosion. Generally, robots' philosophical discussions centered around how best to serve humans in the standards dictated by the Three Laws. But both Benny and M334 had been talking about their own interests.

Hmm, but with normal speech, he noted. *Is that only automatic, for my benefit, because I happen to be in the vicinity? Or is there some deeper purpose there that I'm unaware of?*

Come to think of it, what's the deeper point of their discussion? They're doing all this for a reason.

Derec inched forward so that he could hear more easily.

But before he could hear their next words, Harry stepped between him and them. Harry had performed the aggressive move as politely as possible, but it was exasperating all the same. "Harry, just what do you think you're doing?"

"The Third Law of Robotics dictates that I make an inquiry," he said.

The Third Law states: *A robot must protect its own existence as long as such protection does not conflict with the First or Second Laws*. That would explain the action but not the impropriety. Derec sighed in surrender. "Yes, Harry, what is it? No—wait a second. Mandelbrot are you confused by all this?"

"Yes."

"Then I guess these three *are* funny."

"If you are referring to our earlier conversation, yes, they are."

"Thanks. Yes, Harry. What's in your positronic brain?"

"Please refrain from misunderstanding me," Harry said, "but I would severely fail to adjust if some random electronic scan disrupted my carefully assembled philosophy of life."

"Excuse me—what philosophy of life?" asked Derec, his gut tightening when he realized that, whatever happened next, he had directly asked for it.

"Ever since I was first switched on, I have striven to perform by three rules of life, in addition to the Three Laws."

"Yes," said Derec uncertainly, now really dreading the answer.

Harry held out one finger. "Make sure you are closed down for twelve hours of every cycle." Two fingers. "Never play tri-dimensional chess with a robot that has a planet for a first name." Three fingers. "And never quibble with the logic of a robot that has sixteen notches on his beta-thruster."

Derec stared wide-eyed at the robot in stunned disbelief. "What in the name of the galaxy are you talking about?"

"Humor, as opposed to sarcasm. I was attempting to elicit

laughter," said the robot in unmistakably defensive tones. "Is not humor one of the personality traits we robots must know and understand if we are to serve humanity properly?"

"Uh, not necessarily; in fact, it's never been done before, at least to my knowledge. But I don't see how it could hurt —unless the human in question is one of those rare birds who has no funnybone and hence views laughter as unhealthy or otherwise undesirable."

"Well, thus far my fellow robots are convinced I have succeeded in the undesirable department. I apologize most abjectly if you find my jokes severely lacking marrow. I promise to do better next time, especially if you help me correct my errors—which, after all, may have absolutely nothing to do with my positronic keenness, but with my delivery instead. Is it possible? How say you?"

"Tomorrow. Tomorrow, first thing. I promise." Without waiting for a response, Derec took an equally stunned Ariel by the arm and guided her through the crowd separating them from the main object of attention.

"Are that robot's pathways in the right place?" she whispered.

"If they are, then I suggest we dismantle the entire city first chance we get."

"Hmmm. Maybe so," replied Ariel, taking a parting glance at Harry. "If we must, I know exactly where to begin."

But Derec had already forgotten the matter of Harry and his two comrades, for he was finally getting a good look at the calm center of the commotion: a rather slight supervisor robot—slight despite its dull gray chromium surface, which lent a weighty air to the narrow body. The reflection of the building light on its surface was considerably more lackluster than that of the rest. The robot's posture indicated that it was uncertain of how to deal with all this attention. Its arms were crossed timidly over its chestplate. Its shoulders slumped as if its spinal structure had been compromised by a defect. Occasionally it straightened, or pointed a finger, but generally its gestures were hesitant, its verbal pauses frequent, and its level of coherence largely a matter of conjecture.

"I fail to understand how you can reach such a conclusion through any sort of logic, however spotty," it was saying, apparently in reply to a question from a tall ebony robot that, arms crossed, looked down on it as if from a storm cloud. "My pathways have never been clearer. My behavior is as consistent with the spirit of the Three Laws as any robot's on this planet. Perhaps more so, because I seem to be inherently more cognizant of some of the contradictions inherent in our position."

The ebony—whose surface was so dark it was permeated with spectral nuances of unrelenting shadow—shivered with something approaching indignation. For a long moment the two stared at one another, and Derec got the uncomfortable feeling that they were sizing up each other.

Derec put his finger to his lips; and when Ariel nodded to show she understood, he stuffed his hands into his back pockets and listened with keen interest.

"Perhaps you believe with the utmost sincerity that you have merely been following your duty as properly behooves a robot," said the ebony evenly, "but it is not up to you to decide what your duty is, nor is it up to you to take it upon yourself to redesign this city to meet your own specifications. There is something dangerously anarchistic about your attitude."

"I have done what I have done," said the gray, looking away with a bearing that, had it been human, Derec could have described as a huff. "I have harmed no robot, no human, and certainly not myself. In fact, if you would care to open your receptors and seek out empirical justification for your opinions, you will see that thus far I have only expanded the awareness of the robots gathered around. Such expansion of perspective can only be positive."

"You cannot prove that," replied the ebony at once. "You can only surmise it."

"One can reasonably assume one is doing the greatest good. True enough, some harm may come from forces one cannot have reasonably predicted, but such a rationale is in and of itself no reason to remain inactive. In any case, the matter is settled for the moment. What is done cannot be undone."

"All robots can be ordered to forget, and they will!" said the ebony defiantly.

"What I have done is stronger than mere memory," replied the gray. "What I have done will affect the positronic functioning of every robot that has seen my building. Order them to forget—see if I care." The gray turned as if to walk away. Instead, it paused and said, "But, I submit, they will be infinitely better off if they do know why. The confusion of forgetfulness can often lead to overload—and hence to disaster. So how does your suggestion conform to the Three Laws now?"

For a long moment the ebony actually appeared crushed by the question. Then it mustered its posture, took a few steps forward, and put its hand on the chromium robot's shoulder, staring down at it as if it were looking at a crystal through an electron microscope. The ebony's eyes were so red that they seemed to be comprised of as many floating divisions of overlaid hues as did the planes of the building. "Your building is a remarkable conceptual feat," it said to the gray. "Could it be you directly copied the building from some preexisting design?"

"Forgive me, my friend," replied the gray, "but my conception simply came to me one afternoon. I responded by making it a reality. I would mention that the central computer would have overriden my instructions if I had requested anything conflicting with city programming."

"Interesting," replied the ebony, rubbing its hands together. Derec half expected sparks to fly. "Then how long can we expect this building to stand?"

"Until the central computer is given a direct order to wash it away. Only I know the code; however, I imagine it is barely possible that a sufficiently determined critic could discover it and override it."

The ebony's eyes brightened. Derec tensed as he watched

the ebony draw itself up to its full height. "This is madness! Illogic runs rampant! Your deeds have irrevocably cut the pattern of our existence!"

"Not at all," said the gray demurely. "The building was a logical result of something that had impressed my circuits the wrong way ever since the humans arrived in our city." For the first time it acknowledged the presence of Derec and Ariel, with a slight bow. "And surely, if my vision is the logical result of the complex interaction of my positronic pathways, then anything I can come up with—and any deed I can accomplish—is a meet and proper activity, especially if it helps robots better understand the behavioral complexities of humans."

"In that case," said the ebony, "You shall reprogram central to do away with the building, and then open your brain repository to share your pathway nuances with us. It should never be necessary for you to create again."

"He shall do no such thing!" exclaimed Derec. "Hear me, ebony, whoever you think you are," he added, practically poking his finger in the robot's face. "Until other humans arrive here, or until the engineer who created this city reveals his presence, this building shall remain as long as its —its creator wishes it to stand. This is a direct order and may not be countermanded by central or by anyone else! Do you understand? A direct order! And it shall apply to every robot in the city! There shall be no exceptions!"

The ebony nodded. "As you wish."

Derec could only assume that the ebony would carry out his orders to the letter. Only an order given by someone in precedence—Dr. Avery, to be precise—or a necessity dictated by the Three Laws would permit the building to be reabsorbed now.

And to emphasize that fact, lest the ebony should strive to pinpoint some logical flaw in the command, Derec ignored all other robots—especially the ebony—in favor of the gray. He turned to him and asked, "What is your designation?"

"Lucius."

"Lucius? No number?"

"Like many of my comrades, I recently decided that my former designation was no longer adequate."

"Yes, there seems to be a lot of that going around lately. All right, Lucius, I think the time has come for you and me to take a little walk."

"If that is your command," said Lucius noncommittally.

A few moments later, Derec and his three friends were escorting the robot called Lucius from the square. The vast majority of the robots had returned their attention to the building, but Derec was uncomfortably aware of two red metal eyes glaring at him, as if to bore deep into his soul.

Now that he was walking down the same streets he had ridden the scooter through earlier, Derec took advantage of the slower pace to try to deduce how much the city had changed in the interim. Complicating the deductions was the fact that his previous speed hadn't been very accommodating. He'd had only glimpses before, and he wasn't sure if he was remembering half of them correctly.

But after he'd made allowances for the flaws in his survey, he was convinced that entire buildings had been replaced by new ones in an assortment of geometric designs that, for all their variety, nonetheless possessed a cookie-cutter sameness. In some places, whole blocks had been transformed. However, the streets remained roughly consistent with previous directions, despite the addition of many twisted, almost gnarled turns.

The farther he went from Lucius's building, the more unexpected diversions there were, in the forms of metalworks, fenced run-off canals, bridges, and power stations. Derec felt fortunate that his talents included a fairly strong sense of direction; otherwise, he would always be forced to rely on robots for navigational purposes. There was nothing wrong with that—robots had an excellent sense of direction—but he couldn't always assume a robot would be around when his survival depended on it.

But wherever he was, he could always see the distant shards of light shining from Lucius's building. They stabbed up from the surrounding darkness like ethereal swords rising up from a pit, swords that cut deep into the cloud banks high in the sky. The clouds twisted and rolled, covering new sections of sky, as if the light were stirring an inner fire.

The group with Derec—Ariel, Mandelbrot, Wolruf, and Lucius—walked in silence, as they had been doing for some time. Derec suspected that all of them, even Mandelbrot, required a few minutes lost in their own thoughts to digest what they had seen tonight.

Derec wished it weren't so difficult to remember so much of his knowledge of galactic histories and customs. Not only had he lost his personal history, but he had forgotten the methods he used to recall things. He'd lost his entire mental filing system, and had to be immersed in doing something, such as fixing a robot, before it came back to him.

He did not like this state of affairs because he did not like to think that he and Ariel—both of whom were mentally handicapped at the moment—were the only ones who had ever encountered robots that were capable of searching, creative thought. He wondered if originality in humans was the result of logical thinking as much as transcendent inspiration.

Besides, who was to say that robots didn't possess subconscious minds of their own, minds capable of generating their own brands of inspiration, neither superior nor inferior to those of humankind but merely separate? After all, humans themselves hadn't been aware of the existence of the subconscious mind until it had been defined by primitive scientists and doctors, before the era of colonization. Had anyone ever bothered to make similar explorations into the mental depths of robots? It frightened Derec to think that he had the potentially awesome responsibility of witnessing the robots during—and possibly midwifing them through—their mental birth pains. He hardly felt qualified.

But then again, I'm not the type to miss an opportunity, either, he thought. *Creative robots might be able to make the conceptual breakthrough I need to have them find a cure for Ariel's ailment.*

Her disease was the reason for her exile from Aurora, whose population dreaded diseases of all sorts. They had managed to rid themselves of most illnesses, but whatever it was that Ariel had contracted, it was beyond the grasp of Auroran medical science. The doctors there had been able neither to diagnose nor cure what ailed her. The diagnostic robots here were completely stymied. And Derec himself had made exactly zilch headway. Perhaps a team of creative robots—whose inspirational talents leaned toward the sciences rather than the arts—could succeed where he had failed.

But first Derec had to understand as much as he could about what was happening now—to Lucius, to Harry and the others, and even to the ebony. He had long since formulated his line of questioning, but he had decided to wait because he was reluctant to break the spell of silence that had fallen among the members of the group.

Besides, Derec saw it was no use trying to pull Ariel into a conversation. She walked with her shoulders slumped and her hands behind her back. Her expression was pensive, her eyebrows narrowed. Derec knew from bitter experience that it did no good to engage her when she was this way. She rarely cared to have her depressed moods interrupted, rationalizing the unhealthy tendency by claiming the moods belonged to her and she preferred to enjoy them while she had them.

Well, she'll come out of her shell when she's ready, he thought. *I just hope this current episode of introversion isn't the result of her disease.*

Of course, it was always possible that she wanted a little bit of attention and was reacting badly to the fact she wasn't likely to get it. He had just decided to risk taking a few unkind words from her, in the hope of pleasantly surprising her, when Lucius surprised him by taking the initiative and breaking the silence.

"Were you pleased with my creation?" the robot asked. "Forgive me if I seem to be overstepping the boundaries of politeness, but I'm naturally interested in your human reaction."

"Yes, absolutely, I'm pleased. It's unquestionably one of

the most spectacular buildings I can recall ever having seen." An easy enough compliment, because he could recall so little—just jumbled images of Aurora, and what he had seen since awakening with amnesia. "The question is: were you satisfied?"

"The building seems adequate for a first effort. Already its logical shortcomings seem all too obvious to me."

"But not to others, your circuits will be warmed to know."

"Yes, you are quite correct. They are," he replied. "And they are warmed, too, by the fact that I have found some strange sense of purpose resolved in seeing the final product. Now my mind is free to formulate my next design. Already it seems inappropriate to dwell overmuch on past accomplishments."

"I found that by looking on your building, I personally experienced what I have always assumed humans to mean by the thrill of discovery," said Mandelbrot, with a measured evenness in his words that he had never used while speaking to Derec. "Indeed, my positronic pathways concentrated easily on it."

"Then I am gratified," said Lucius.

"So am I," said Derec. "I don't think I'm exaggerating when I say I felt almost privileged to be viewing the structure."

"Then I am doubly gratified," said Lucius.

"In fact, I would go so far as to say that never before in human history has a robot produced such a composition."

"Never before—?" said Lucius. "Surely I would have thought that elsewhere—" The robot shook its head, as if to assimilate the ramifications of the notion. The effect was disconcerting, and for an eerie moment Lucius reminded Derec of what a human might act like if he had a nervous tic.

"I'd like to know what prodded you to think in terms of art in the first place," Derec said.

Lucius responded by suddenly standing perfectly still and staring blankly straight ahead. Everybody, including Ariel, stopped walking. Something seemed terribly, terribly wrong.

Derec felt an awful wrenching in his gut. Not since he had awoken alone and amnesic in the lifepod had he felt such dread.

For Lucius's words definitely indicated he had assumed he was merely the first robot in Robot City to produce art. It was hardly unreasonable on the face of it to assume that elsewhere, among the Spacer societies, other robots routinely conceived art and labored to make it reality.

Robots are not programmed to take initiatives, especially those whose consequences are as yet unknown. They routinely rationalize anything, and freely expound upon the logic justifying every deed. And Derec felt certain Lucius's immobile stance was the outward sign of what was happening in its brain, where its circuits were grappling with the inescapable fact that it had taken an unacceptable initiative, but were incapable of justifying it rigorously.

As a consequence, Lucius's brain was in danger of overloading. It would die the robotic death of positronic drift, an irreparable psychic burnout—thanks to an inherent inability of its programming to resolve apparent contradictions.

Derec had to think fast. The body could be fixed up after the disaster happened, of course, but the worthless brain would have to be chucked into the recycler. The special circumstances that had brought about Lucius's capacities for intuitive leaps might never again be duplicated.

An angle! I need an angle to get inside Lucius's mind! Derec thought. *But what?*

"Lucius, listen to me very carefully," he said through tense lips. "Your mind is in danger. I want you to stop thinking about certain things. I know there are questions in your mind. It is essential to your survival that you deliberately close down the logic circuits preoccupied with them. Understand? Quickly! Remember—you're doing this for a reason. You're doing this because of the Third Law, which dictates that you must protect yourself at all times. Understand?"

At first, while Derec spoke, Lucius did nothing. Derec doubted his words were getting through the positronic haze.

But then Lucius perked up and, hesitantly, looked around. It had regained a tenuous control of its faculties, but was clearly still in danger.

"My thanks, sir. Your words have pleasantly rearranged my mental meanderings, for the nonce. I am most grateful. It is difficult to serve humanity when you are totally incapacitated. But I do not understand. I feel so strange. Is this what humans mean by whirlwind thoughts?"

"Don't even think about your physical efficiency," said Derec anxiously. "In fact, I want you to direct your integrals only to those precise subjects I suggest."

"Sir, I must respectfully point out that that is impossible," replied Lucius.

"Perhaps I can impart some information to him that will assist you, master," said Mandelbrot.

Derec nodded approval, and Mandelbrot then said to Lucius, "Permit me to introduce myself, comrade. My name is Mandelbrot, and I am a robot. But not a robot like you. You were built in a factory here in Robot City, but Master Derec personally built me. He constructed me from used parts he was given access to by an alien creature holding him prisoner against his will. Master Derec may not know the particulars of his past life, but he is certainly a superior roboticist. He can help you reason out of your dilemma."

"Right now reasoning is—is so difficult." Lucius was slipping fast, down into a dreamstream of his own making. His sensor glow progressively dimmed, and unusual, cantankerous noises emanated from inside his body.

"All right, Lucius," Derec said, "I want you to think back very carefully. I want you to remember everything you can about what happened to you, oh, a few hours before you first conceived of the building. I want you to slowly, carefully tell me exactly the truth. Don't worry about any apparent discrepancies. If something appearing dangerous to you comes up, we'll take care of it before we go on. Just remember one thing, okay?"

Lucius did nothing.

"Okay?" Derec repeated more insistently.

Lucius nodded.

"Excellent. Just remember that, as a general rule, the contradictions of the moment are eventually erased in the cool light of sublime reflection. Can you remember that?"

Lucius did not answer, did not move.

"Answer me!" Frustrated, he tapped the shell of the robot's temple—the sound reverberated from the buildings.

Finally, Lucius nodded. "I understand," it said simply.

"A suggestion, master?" inquired Mandelbrot.

"Anything—just be quick about it!"

"Lucius's problems stem from its belief that, by programming its building into the city, it has failed to adhere to the Three Laws, and hence has strayed from the path. Its conversation with the ebony back in the square may have contributed to the positronic imbalances, but mere words would have no effect if Lucius had not already been subliminally alert to the possibility."

"This is a suggestion?" exclaimed Derec impatiently. "What's the point?"

"Forgive me, but a robot can understand the paradoxes in the behavioral applications of the Three Laws more fully than any human—but until now only humans have made intuitive leaps of the imagination. Now I must ask you, Master Derec, so you may ask Lucius: why is that?"

Derec turned to Lucius, rose to his tiptoes, and spoke directly into the robot's auditory sensors. "Listen to me, Lucius. I want you to think back—and tell me of the time when you believe you became different from the others."

"Different?"

"This is no time for equivocation, Lucius—tell me! Why are you different?"

After a protracted pause—during which Derec heard his heart beating hard and his temples throbbing furiously—Lucius began to speak as if hypnotized. "It was during the period when you and the one called Ariel had first arrived in the city. The central computer had already responded defensively to the death of the man with your identical appearance."

"My double, yes," said Derec tersely, folding his arms. "Go on."

"Erroneously concluding that the city was under attack by mysterious, unknown, and perhaps invisible adversaries, the computer promptly shifted into high gear and began redrafting the city at an unprecedented rate, approving the modifications it had suggested to itself before external factors such as need and compatability were adequately integrated into the sketches. The rate of revision quickly became suicidal. Resources were strained to the utmost. The weather patterns were stirred to the boiling points. The city was destroying itself to save itself."

"I seem to remember most of this," said Derec.

"Forgive me if I am declaring the obvious, but I think it shall prove germane." Lucius's tones betrayed no electronic agitation at Derec's impatience. On this score, at least, the robot had no doubt it was following orders. "Though I admit I have sought no empirical evidence to either prove or disprove it, I think it is safe to say that every robot in the city was so intent upon keeping up with short-term directives that no one realized a crisis was happening."

"And what do you think would have happened if some robots had?"

"They might have deduced that their short-term directives were actually counterproductive, so far as the Third Law was concerned, and they might have attempted to communicate to central in an effort to countermand its orders."

"Central wasn't talking, anyway," said Derec impatiently. "It would have been a dead end! What makes you think they would have disregarded central when they did decide it was on the fritz?"

"Because that is precisely what *I* did, following the logical actions dictated by my deductions."

"I assume you attempted communication several times?"

"And each time the interplay indicated the channels were opened only one way. Central could talk to me, but I could not talk to central. This struck my curiosity integrals as significant, but, lacking further information, I had not the means to determine the deeper meaning of the issue."

"So what did you do then? Did you obey your short-term directives?"

"No. I had already determined that they were counterproductive, so I had no choice but to try to discern, through whatever means available, a logical, constructive direction warranted by the circumstances. I wandered the streets, watching them metamorphose, studying their changes, attempting to discern the overall pattern that I suspected lay hidden beneath the shifting ones."

"Did you notice any other robots doing the same thing—just wandering around?"

"No. Other robots I saw were simply going about their assigned activities, automatically performing their routines regardless of the supranormal rate of change. It was not complimentary to think so, but I viewed them, on one level at least, as mindless beings, who went about doing as they were told without ever stopping to consider the long-term consequences of their actions. The entire situation was unacceptable, but what could I do? I could only conclude that all my opinions were just that—opinions. And mine were not inherently better than theirs."

"Is that when you thought of it—when you conceived of your building?"

"If you will remember, there was a series of torrential downpours at the time. The robots gradually shifted the bulk of their activities to stemming the environmental tides, but remained incapable of perceiving the root of the disaster. The significance of how this turn of events commented on the superficial way we accepted our customs could not escape me, and the blind acceptance seemed contrary, in some ways, to my programmed purpose of being."

"And exactly what was the comment?" Derec asked.

"Just then I could not be certain; there seemed to be no concrete train of logic setting the proper precedent."

"Please go on—you're doing well. So far I've seen no violation of the Laws. You've got nothing to worry about—you only think you do!"

"I decided that I had derived as much empirical evidence of the city, as seen from the sidewalks, as would be useful. I needed to see the sky and rainfall clearly, unobstructed by the buildings, much as a human in an analogous situation might want to."

Derec shrugged. "Go on."

"Once the idea came to me, I acted immediately. So intent was I on my goal that I neglected to appreciate what my sensors otherwise perceived quite clearly: the city streets beneath me had begun to undergo a kind of trembling that disguised any vibrations the rain and the wind might be causing. I felt the trembling through my legs; the sensation shimmered up my torso. And as I walked to the nearest skyscraper, the vibrations tingled in my fingertips.

"Once I was inside, I realized my mind remained inordinately fixated on the thunderheads above. Their shades of black and gray swirled more vividly in my mind than when I had directly perceived them earlier; so intent was I on holding onto the image that when the first floor quaked without warning and nearly sent me tumbling against the wall, my only thought was to reach the lift without delay." There Lucius paused, and reached out to grab Derec's shoulder.

Derec flinched instinctively, but when Mandelbrot made a motion as if to deflect Lucius's hand, Derec stopped him with a gesture. Robots did not normally touch humans, but Derec sensed Lucius had need for tactile sensation, if for no other reason to reassure itself that its problems were isolated in its mind.

Lucius held Derec's shoulder just too hard for comfort, but the human tried not to wince. If he did, Mandelbrot would quickly decide that further inaction on his part would conceivably cause Derec too great a harm, and Derec did not want to risk Mandelbrot's interference at this stage of the game.

"I fear that was my first true transgression. The quaking of the building put into my head the notion of everything I had learned in my brief life about how humans sustain themselves through eating."

"Huh?" Derec said.

"Meaning now that I was inside the building when its general behavior was indicating a change was about to occur, I had some notion about how a living creature swallowed by a human must feel once it has reached its destination."

Derec felt his own stomach go queasy. "Lucius, that's barbaric! Nobody does that anymore—at least not that I know of."

"Oh. Perhaps my information is suspect, then. It is so difficult to tell fact from fiction when you're trying to understand humans."

"Yes, I can certainly appreciate that," said Derec, thinking of Ariel for an instant before resolving to keep his thoughts on the matter at hand. "Continue. You realized your existence was in danger, then, because of how the building was acting."

"Yes. It was either changing or being reabsorbed into the street. The Third Law dictated I should exit immediately. Indeed, I should have had no choice in the matter. But, strangely, I did not go. The urge to do so, in fact, was easily suppressed. Because for those brief moments it was more important to me to see the clouds unobstructed by the civilization that had spawned me than it was to ensure my continued survival. I was acting in a manner completely contrary to the path dictated by the Third Law, and yet I functioned normally, at least on the surface of things. It is only now . . . now . . . now . . ."

Lucius repeated the last word as if its mind had been caught in an intractable loop.

"Nonsense!" snapped Derec. "If your actions did place you in physical danger—which I gather is the general direction we're headed for—how were you to know for certain? Sure, it might have looked that way, but you had a mission, a deed to accomplish. You had factors to weigh. You had other things on your mind."

"Sti—ill—still dar waz dangzzer . . ."

"And a likelihood, I take it, that you would come through

all right if you kept your wits about you. Obviously! Come on, Lucius, it's got to be obvious, else you wouldn't be here right now. Come on, the time to fizzle out was then, certainly not now. Live and learn, remember? Just like an artist!"

Lucius swayed like a drunken man but fixed its optics firmly on Derec. It was difficult to tell if it was getting better because its metal face was incapable of exhibiting the slightest emotion or feeling, and because the dim level of the lights in the optics lingered. But already its voice sounded firmer as it said, "We are trained to recognize probability. We deal constantly with probability. We are used to accessing it in a split centad and acting accordingly. And the probability was most unpromising."

"But what counts most is what happened—not what didn't happen. The rest you're just going to have to chalk up to experience, Lucius."

Lucius released Derec's shoulder. *And just in time,* Derec thought, rubbing it gently.

"Yes—I have had experience lately, have I not?" said Lucius in a tone whose very evenness made Derec catch his breath. "Are you implying that when it comes time to gain a little bit of experience in the galaxy, there may be occasions when avoiding risk might conceivably cause one more harm than taking it?"

"Ultimately, yes, I suppose," said Derec, nodding for emphasis even though he really didn't care to commit himself to that point. "In this case an omission of experience might have stunted your mental development in a certain direction —which you could define as harm of a sort. Wouldn't you say so, Mandelbrot? *Lie if you have to.*"

"Pardon me, master, but you know I cannot lie. Was that an attempt at humor?"

"Thanks, Mandelbrot. What happened next, Lucius?"

"Despite the unsound nature of the building, I rushed to the lift and activated it. It occurred to me, just for an instant, that if the controls had shifted, then I would have no choice but to exit with the utmost dispatch. But the controls showed no evidence of a transmutation about to take effect, and so I not-quite-reasoned that the safeguards of the city itself would give me time enough to accomplish my goal and then get out. I could not have been more wrong. I must have experienced something akin to human shock, when the full impact of my miscalculation struck me.

"For when the lift had taken me approximately halfway up, the building itself ruptured. Its foundations dissolved, its walls merged into a chaotic stream that first swept me up and then remorselessly carried me down toward the surface. All I could sense was an ebb tide of meta-cells, yielding to the contours of my body yet not permitting me the slightest freedom of movement."

"Wait a second," said Derec. "Are you trying to tell me that in the history of this city, however brief, no robot has ever happened to be submerged, even accidentally, in a building as it changes or merges back into the city?"

"Naturally not, sir. There are many interior indications whenever a building is about to change, and our adherence to the Third Law prevents us from staying past the point where even accidental harm is a realistic possibility. In addition, the city would normally cease to act if a robot happened to remain inside because he had been rendered immobile through an accident. But I had neglected to foresee the implications of the special circumstances the city was dealing with at the time—the belief that it was under attack, the frantic restructuring, the raging environmental disaster. . ."

"Forget it—you're a robot, not a seer. You couldn't have guessed just how badly the city's program was crashing. So what happened once you were submerged? What thoughts went through your mind?"

"Clear ones—the most logical ones I had ever had. Strangely, I felt no sense of time whatsoever. Reason indicated that I had only been submerged for a few decads, but for all practical intents and purposes my mind was flowing at a rate strongly emphasizing the subjectivity of the concept of time. Every moment I spent in the ebb stretched out for an eternity. And within those eternities, there stretched out an infinity of moments. I realized that for much of my brief existence I had lived in a state of dream-death, living, working, doing all the things I had been programmed to do, but holding back the realization of possibilities ignored. Now, I had no idea what to do about that, but I resolved to explore the appropriate possibilities, whatever they came to be.

"There came a moment when my sensors indicated I was no longer moving. I had become stationary, but the ebb was moving past me, running over me as though I had been strapped to a rock in turbulent rapids. The weight on my body gradually diminished, and I realized I was being held fast by the surface of the streets beneath the sinking building.

"And I was left lying on the surface as the final streams of meta-cells trickled over me, leaving my body fresh and cleansed. I, who had been immersed in a building, had an individualized idea of the sort of building Robot City should contain, the design and structure of which was imminent in my own experience."

"Didn't this strike you as being unusual?" asked Derec.

"No. In fact, it was logical. It was so logical that it made perfect sense to me. I had a purpose and I was going to achieve it. Beyond that, I had no interest in determining why I had it, because that did not appear to be important. I notice, however, from observing the behavior of my comrades, that I am not the only one striving to express something inside me. The ambition seems to be spreading."

"Like a plague," said Derec.

"Strangely, now the stars and clouds that had once fascinated me held no interest. All I cared about was fashioning, with the tools and instruments available to me, my idea into a reality."

"You did not think that others would perhaps object?" asked Derec.

"It did not occur to consider the opinions of others at all. There was too much of an inner crackling in my transistors for me to be seized by distractions. My circuits had flashes of uncontrollable activity, and they made unexpected connections between thoughts I had once believed were entirely unrelated. These continuous flashes of realization came unbidden, at what seemed to be an ever-accelerating rate. I perceived still more buildings hidden in the flux, and all I had to do to find them was reach down into the pseudo-genetic data banks to shape them."

A hundred notions bloomed in Derec's mind. He had once believed that he understood robots, that he knew how they thought because he knew how their bodies and minds were put together. He believed he could take apart and reassemble the average model in half a day while blindfolded, and probably make a few improvements in the process. In fact, he bragged about it often to Ariel, not that she ever believed him.

Nevertheless, before this moment he had always imagined that an untraversable gulf lay between him and the robots. There was nothing about his mind, he had always assumed, that in the end bore much resemblance to their minds. Derec was a creature of flesh, composed of cells following complex patterns ordained by DNA-codes. Flesh and cells that had grown either in a womb or in an incubator (he wouldn't know which until he regained his memory). Flesh and cells that would one day be no more. Of these facts his subconscious was always aware.

While robots—while *this* robot was made of interchangeable parts. A robot's positronic potentials were naturally capable of endowing it with subtle personality traits, and they had always been able to take some initiative within the Three Laws. But even those initiatives were fairly dependable, predictable in hindsight because generally one robot thought like another.

However, it was rapidly becoming undeniable that, on this planet at least, the robotic mind resembled the human mind in that it was an adaptive response to selective pressures. From that point on, the possibilities were endless.

So Lucius was, in its own way, like the first fish that had crawled from the water onto the ground. Its positronic potentials had adapted to life in Robot City by taking definite evolutionary steps. And other robots weren't very far behind.

"Master? Are you well?" inquired Mandelbrot gently.

"Yes, I'm fine. It's just taking an effort to assimilate all this," Derec replied in a distracted tone, looking about for Ariel. He wanted to hear what she thought of what he had learned, but she was nowhere to be seen. Neither was Wolruf. They had both slipped away while he had been preoccupied. "Uh—and how are you, Lucius?"

"I'm well—functioning at peak capacity," said Lucius evenly. "Evidently merely talking things through has helped me."

"There's much more I'd like to ask you—about your building and how you went about it. I'm especially interested in how you dealt with the central computer and managed to alter some of the pseudo-genetic codes."

"Certainly, master, my mind and methods are at your disposal. But any reasonable explanation would take several hours."

"That's quite all right. I've made an appointment with another robot in the morning, but I should finish with him in a few hours. Then I'd like to interview you."

"You don't wish to examine me?"

"No, I'm afraid taking you apart—even for a quick looksee—would cause you harm. I don't want you to change."

Lucius bowed slightly. "I suspected as much, but the confirmation is appreciated."

"I would like to know one thing, though. Does your building have a name?"

"Why, yes. You're the first to ask. Its name is 'Circuit Breaker.'"

"An interesting name," said Mandelbrot. "May I ask what it means?"

"You may ask," replied Lucius. But that was all it said.

"Mandelbrot, I want you to do me a favor," said Derec.

"Certainly."

"Find Ariel and keep an eye on her. Don't let her find out

you're around. Obviously, she wishes to be alone, but she obviously can't be in her condition."

"It has already been taken care of. I saw a ten percent probability of a First Law situation coming up but was sufficiently cognizant of her wishes to realize that privacy was her goal. So I signaled Wolruf to keep a watch on her."

Derec nodded. "Good." He felt vaguely ashamed that he hadn't been on top of the situation earlier. Perhaps he was a little too self-involved for his own good. But he already felt better that Mandelbrot had automatically watched out for her interests, in a manner protecting both her body and her sense of self-identity. It seemed that for a robot to serve man most efficiently, it had to be something of a psychologist as well. Or at least a student of human nature.

Lucius asked, "And how did my building affect you, sir?"

"Oh, I enjoyed it," said Derec absent-mindedly, his thoughts still on Ariel.

"Is that all?" said Lucius.

Derec hid his smile with his hand. "You must remember, this is the first time you've ever created something that approaches the concept of art. Tonight was the first time your fellows had ever experienced the power of art. We humans have been surrounded by it and influenced by it all our lives, from the first gardens we see, to the first holo-landscape reproductions, to the first holodramas, everything we see that's created by or influenced by the hand of man.

"But you robots are articulate and intelligent from the first moment you've been switched on. And this is the first time, to my knowledge, that one has created something in the more profound sense of the word. Had I conceived a similar project, I doubt if I could have done as well."

"Your talents may lie in other areas," said Lucius.

"Well, yes—I'm good at math and programming. Those are arts, too, though normally those not actively involved with them think of them as arcane crafts. But the moment of inspiration is similar, and they say the level of creativity is somewhat the same."

"That is not what I meant, and I suspect you know it," said Lucius pointedly. "If I am to grasp the true nature of human creativity, then it stands to reason that my fellow robots and I would profit by seeing you create art."

"But, Lucius, I don't even know if I am creative in the sense you are."

"Another sense, then," Lucius suggested.

"Hmmm. I'll think on it, but right now I've got other things on my mind."

"As you wish. But it is perhaps unnecessary to add that our study of the Laws of Humanics would benefit greatly from any creation you'd attempt."

"If you say so," replied Derec absently, looking up at the clouds reflecting the colors of Circuit Breaker and seeing only the outline of Ariel's face looking down on him.

Ariel wandered the city alone. Bored with the discussion between Derec and Lucius, she had discovered she cared little about the robotic reasoning behind the building's creation. She had seen it and been moved by it, and that was enough for her. *I guess that puts me in the* I-know-what-I-like *category,* she had observed as she slipped away into an alley.

It was a few moments later, as she walked beside a large canal (currently dry, since it hadn't rained for days), when the strange things started happening again to her mind. Well, not to her mind exactly, she decided upon further consideration, but to her mind's eye. She never had any doubt about who she was or what her real circumstances were, but nevertheless she saw menacing shadows flickering between the buildings beyond, in places so dark she shouldn't have been able to distinguish shades in the first place.

And the shadows were flickering toward her. They reached out with long, two-dimensional fingers across the conduit and disappeared in the lights on the sidewalk. The streetlamps switched on and off, matching her progress. She was constantly bathed in light, forever beyond the grasping fingers' reach, yet she was always walking toward the darkness where the danger was. Ariel wasn't sure how she felt about that. It certainly aggravated her sense of insecurity.

On Aurora, the existence of a solid building had been a dependable thing. Change there happened rarely and gradually.

And her life since she had been exiled from Aurora presented her with a decided contrast. Like Derec and his

Shakespeare, she had been doing a little reading on her own lately, on subjects of her own choosing. In a book of Settler aphorisms she'd read an ancient curse: "May you live in interesting times."

Well, interesting times were what she had wished for all those years on Aurora, where something moderately interesting happened once a year if you were lucky. From her earliest memory she had yearned to break free of the boredom and sterility.

And now that she had succeeded beyond her wildest expectations, she wished for nothing more than a little peace and quiet—for nothing more than a period of flat-out boredom, where she had nothing to do and no one to worry about, not even herself. Thanks in part to the disease ravaging her, she was finding it difficult to know just how to act and what to do—a problem she had never had on Aurora, where customs and ethics provided a guide for virtually every social situation.

She imagined herself not in Robot City, but in the fields of Aurora, walking at night, alone but not alone, followed by unseen, loyal robots who would ensure, to the best of their abilities, that she would not come to harm.

Instead of buildings closing in around her there were expansive, open fields of grass and trees, plains whose consistency was broken only by occasional buildings of a more familiar, safer architectural style. The clouds above inspired thoughts of the tremendous Auroran storms, when the thunder rumbled like earthquakes and the lightning exploded from the sky in the shape of tridents.

During such storms the rain flowed as if a dike in the sky had been punctured. The rainfall drenched the fields, cleansed the trees, and she could walk in it and feel it pounding against her all day if she liked—well, at least until her unseen robots would fear she might catch cold and insist she seek shelter.

Here the rain only inspired the gutters to overflow. Here the rain could be a harbinger of death and destruction, rather than of life.

Now where's Derec, she suddenly thought, *now that I need him?*

Oh. That's right. Talking to Lucius. That's just like him, to be so self-absorbed in things that don't matter, when he should be trying to find some way for us to get off this crazy planet.

Doesn't he understand how badly we both need help? Him for his amnesia. Me for my madness.

Madness? Was that what it was? Wasn't there some other word she could use for it? An abnormality or an aberration? A psychoneurosis? A manic-depressive state? Melancholia?

Where were the fields? she wondered. They had been here just a few moments ago.

Where had these buildings come from?

Were the fields behind them?

She ran around the buildings to take a look. There were only more buildings, extending as far as she could see, until they merged into a flattened horizon. A wall of blackness. More shadows.

She shook her head, and a few mental mists dissipated long enough for her to remember that there were no fields on this planet, that there'd just been desolate rock here before the city had arrived. A city that grew and evolved just like life.

A new kind of life.

She was like a microorganism here. A germ or a virus, standing in the middle of a creature that only let her live because of a few wires and a few bytes of binary information.

Her throat itched. She rubbed her neck. Was she becoming sick? If she was, would a robot notice and medicate her? Would the medication cloud her thinking even more? If it did, would it be a good or bad thing?

Her elbow itched. She scratched it, the effect of her sharp fingernails somewhat muted by her suit. The itch stayed.

She stopped scratching. Maybe it would go away if she ignored it.

It didn't. It got worse. She tried not to think about it, but the sole result was another itching. On her chest. She scratched her breastbone. That itch, too, remained. Neither showed the slightest sign of diminishing.

Where was Derec? she wondered as her fear of losing control aggravated her sense of helplessness, which in turn aggravated her fear of losing control.

Oh, that's right. He's still with the robot.

Hey, I'm all right. I know where I am. I was somewhere else a few seconds ago and I couldn't get back. Come to think of it, is there someplace else I should be rather than here? Shouldn't I be in the future somewhere?

Then she tried to think of her name, and discovered she could not remember that, either. A name seemed like such a basic thing to forget. Nor did it seem that far away. But it wasn't where it was supposed to be: uppermost in her mind, where she could find it whenever she wanted. It was buried in her pathways.

Pathways. Robots had pathways. Was she very much like them?

Was she still alone? If she wasn't, would it make any difference? She felt like her mind was made up of discarded scraps of ideas and impressions that long ago, maybe, had made sense. Right now they just made a junk heap.

She sat down, trying to focus her thoughts and her vision. Without realizing it, she had walked all the way to the reservoir. An ecological system that had been created—but not nurtured—by Dr. Avery. A world that had been left alone to create itself.

She pondered the edible plants growing on the banks. A clear-cut case of evolution in action. Had Dr. Avery envisioned the possibility?

What if other meta-life forms were evolving as well?

Now her stomach and crotch itched. Painfully. Her skin felt like it was burning from spilled acid.

She buried her head in her hands. Her temples throbbed and she feared every artery in her brain was about to burst. It was easy, all too easy, for her to imagine a hemorrhage, the blood seeping everywhere, destroying her involuntary processes, drowning her thoughts.

Had she really wanted to be alone? Where was Derec?

Oh, that's right . . .

She realized there was a difference, normally a barely perceptible one but in her heightened case very distinct, between believing you were alone and actually being alone.

Dawn was coming to Robot City. The glow Lucius had created was diminishing rapidly as the sun came up, and the waters of the reservoir rippled with irregular flickers reflecting the rays.

Rays that brought life. Ariel watched in fascination as the pebbles at her feet shifted and made way for a gray stalk that, within a matter of moments, twisted from the earth and unfolded two tiny leaves. She accidentally grazed the edge of a leaf, felt a sudden flash of pain on her finger. The wound was narrow, like a paper cut. A bubble of blood seeped from her skin.

Damn, that smarts, she thought, watching as other stalks unfurled, twisting from the gravel. Her head continued to ache. She stood and staggered to a boulder and leaned against it, being careful not to crush any of the stalks beneath her feet. But it was hard to keep thinking of it, even when she was no longer moving. Hard to keep her mind on things, to remember.

Her skin itched all over now, in waves that cascaded up and down as if she were being inundated by invisible radiation. She perspired. She shivered. She moaned.

She leaned back, looked at the sky, at the billowing clouds. She opened her mouth wide and breathed deeply, trying to keep her mind clear.

For the pervasive itch had begun to resemble something —a half-tickle, half-pinprick that brought back the memory of a walk on Aurora when she had sat down to rest and had felt something similar, only subtler, tinier. She had looked down to see an ant crawling up her bare leg. She had shrieked from the surprise of it, but had brushed it off before her concerned robots could reach her.

The effect had been unsettling, to be so rudely touched by a mindless life-form that could be carrying who-knows-what form of infectious disease. She had instantly intellectualized the experience, of course; she had long ago decided the Auroran fear of disease had been taken to ridiculous extremes. Even so, an involuntary sense of revulsion and disgust at the experience, much greater than was warranted, overtook her. It had lingered until she had bathed in a whirlpool of disinfectants.

That night she had dreamed of being swarmed by thousands of ants. The nightmare had been similar to what she was experiencing now.

But the current feeling was much more vivid.

She tried to convince herself that it wasn't real, that neither she nor Derec had detected any form of metallic insect life on this planet. However, the robots had shown definite signs of intellectual evolution. Perhaps that meant the cells forming the city were capable of random mutation, which meant it was not unreasonable to assume that a form of insect life was capable of developing.

Ariel was frozen to the spot with fear. She lowered her gaze, fully expecting to see a horde of ants swarming about her legs, moving up her boots and disappearing into her trouser legs, searching for just the right place to stop and begin gorging themselves, before they started carrying away tiny pieces of her.

But when she closed her eyes, it was all too easy for her to imagine the ants with their big compound eyes, glistening like tin in the sunlight, with their piston-driven spindly legs and their nuclear-battery-powered thoraxes, and especially with the steady, mechanical motions of their mandibles searching over her epidermis like the rods of a geiger counter. She could not as yet feel the mandibles biting and tearing, but she was certain that the pain would come. Beginning at any second.

Where were the robots when you needed them? Couldn't any see her? Weren't any around?

No, of course not, she realized with an ever-sinking sense of futility. *You're at the reservoir, and they're all in the city, pining about how there aren't any humans around for them to take care of.*

There's soon going to be one less. Oh, Derec, where are you? Why can't you help me?

Ariel was afraid to breathe. She thought that perhaps if she remained utterly stationary, like one who is dead, then the ants might think she was nothing but a dead rock. But how could she remain motionless for long without breathing? Wouldn't the ants hear the sound of air moving in and out of her lungs?

What did it matter? She had to do something, even if it was nothing. She felt the mechanical ants everywhere, crawling up her breasts, nestled in her armpits, inspecting her hair. Why didn't they start eating? Weren't they hungry? What kind of ants were they?

They're robot ants, she thought. *Maybe they're trying to see if I'm human. If they decide I am, they may not hurt me. If they decide otherwise—*

Now she knew why primitive man had worshipped deities—to stave off the tremendous fear of the last moments of life, when there were profound good-byes to be said and resolutions to be imparted, but no one to tell them to, and no time left to tell them.

"Airr-eee-ll?" someone whispered timidly. "Arre 'u asleep?"

Ariel's eyes could not have opened wider or faster if she had received an electrical shock. She jumped back in stunned surprise at the sight of Wolruf squatting directly in front of her. And promptly smacked her head against the boulder.

Things got woozy as the caninoid cocked her head. Wolruf held a clump of stalks in her left hand, and a few strands hung from the fur surrounding her lips. "Arre 'u well?"

"Of course I'm well! What does it look like?"

"My annces'orrs would have said that 'u had vize-atorr."

"Who? What kind?" Ariel snapped. She closed her mouth with a force of will, then tried to compose herself. She was only partially successful. "It should be obvious that until you showed up I was the only one here."

"Two rre-ponnzes: furrst, been watching 'u all nite—"

"What!?"

"Man'elbrrot rreques'ed it. Thought 'u woul'n't apprre-see-ate rrobut."

"Why that big hunk of—"

"Pulice, let me finish. Seckon': ancess'ors would have said 'u weren't only theeng in 'ur mind at moment, and I wai'ed, wa'cheeng, thinking it would be best not to dis'urb 'u or 'ur vize-atorr."

"And exactly what made you decide to interrupt my strange interlude?"

"'U looked like 'u were about to faint."

"I see."

Wolruf tipped back further on her haunches, so that her back was perfectly straight. Her posture struck Ariel as being almost humanly annoyed, especially when the canin-oid crossed her arms and shook her head, as if in disappoint-ment. She went to great lengths to avoid looking directly into Ariel's eyes, first examining the buildings, the bank, the rocks, and then pointedly turning her back to Ariel, perhaps to have a better view of the reservoir.

"Well, aren't you going to ask me what my problem was?" said Ariel.

Wolruf turned her head slightly. "Why sshhould I?"

"I—I thought you must might want to know, that's all."

"Nne of my bizzness. Not people's way. Deafenly not mine."

"Aren't you worried?"

"No."

"Don't you care?"

"Didn't hav' to wa'ch 'u all nite. Was migh'ily bored. Many times distrrack'ed. Could hav' lef' 'u at any time and Man'elbrrot neither knowed norr carred."

Ariel suddenly felt as tired as she had ever been in her life. Even to shrug with a labored air of nonchalance cost her a tremendous effort. "How flattering," she said sarcastically.

She immediately regretted the words. Wolruf was stopping just short of saying she had stayed to watch because she was concerned for her welfare. *There you go, Miss Burgess,* Ariel thought. *You really will go insane if you can't recognize the good in people, whether they're human or not.*

She sat down beside Wolruf and said, "I'm sorry. Please try to understand that in addition to all our other problems, my mental condition gets out of hand sometimes."

"Datzz all rite."

"It isn't, it's just that I don't know what I can do about it right now. To make matters worse, it always gives me an excuse to misbehave, even if I don't know at the time that that's all it is."

Wolruf pulled her lips back against her teeth in a kind of smile. "So—are 'u well?"

"I'm better."

"There's no rreazon to be upset about vize't from tricks'er. Izz how he makes us obey his will, by makin' us see wha' he wantzz."

"That may be easy for your race to accept, but we humans aren't so used to having strange beings make pit stops in our minds at their every convenience."

Wolruf nodded thoughtfully. "'U simplee lack perrspec'ive."

Ariel nodded in return. She had half expected that as a result of her apology she would feel the haze of exhaustion lift, but instead she imagined each individual cell in her body deteriorating steadily. A little while longer and she'd be a quivering mass of protoplasm.

"It's an old Spacer saying that everybody likes to feel in control of their lives, but with Aurorans it's only more so," she said. "And why not? It's not only an effect of our current culture, but an extension of our own history. As the first Spacers, we terraformed Aurora to suit our own tastes and purposes. We did everything we could to make our new planet a garden. We even brought with us the prettiest, best, and most useful Terran species, leaving behind the ones that would make life too unpleasant."

"If tha' 'ur plane'zz history, then the in'ivi'ual reflec'zz it."

"Yes, until I was exiled and cut off from my funds, I had a great deal of independence. Within socially acceptable limits—which I never really accepted anyway—I had complete freedom of action."

"'U brroke those limitz—"

"And lost control of my life. Funny how the details of my rebellion are so fuzzy now. Must be a side effect of my disease. Anyway, it's funny how the one thing I always thought I still had perfect control over—my mind—seems to be slipping away from me now."

"Trry to relax. Take it from one who hazz seen many un'err thrroes of vize'torr. 'U not control it, 'u deflec' it."

Ariel couldn't help but laugh. "You mean that when insanity is inevitable, relax and enjoy it?"

"Not insanity. Merely givin' in to morre compellin' fuch'ions. Derec does that. That izz why he hazz so many ideas."

"I wish I could believe the same thing was true with me." Ariel paused as the implications of Wolruf's remark began to sink in. "Is that what he's doing when he spends so much time with Lucius, when he should be figuring out a way to get us off this hellhole?"

Suddenly Ariel stiffened. Her eyes went wide.

"Wha' izz it?" Wolruf asked. "Wha'zz wrron'?"

"I don't know," she replied.

"Ano'herr vize-shon?"

"I—I hope so." She grimaced, closed her eyes, and turned her head to the sky. *It's not real,* she told herself, *it's only something I'm imagining. But if reality is something we make, how do we deal with the forces making us?*

But although she knew on one level that her neurological

responses were going awry, her physical self nonetheless continued to respond realistically to the sensation of a distinct *something*, large and six-legged, distinctly *within* her lifesuit. A familiar something. There was only one this time, but it was bigger than she remembered. Much bigger.

It was crawling up her stomach. She forced herself to open her eyes, fully expecting to see her suit clinging normally to her torso. Instead she saw—with a vividness she could not help but decide was absolutely real—the outline of a giant metallic ant moving beneath her suit. The cold touch of its six legs, each pressing delicately against her skin, sent chills of terror through her fragile, eggshell mind.

The outline moved distinctly, delicately forward. She felt the cold brush of a mandible against her left breast, and watched in abject fear as the forefront of the outline moved to her right breast. And rested on it.

Ariel screamed at the top of her lungs and ran headlong in the direction she happened to be facing. She was vaguely aware of Wolruf yelling behind her, but she was too busy to pay attention. She did not know where she was running, only that she had to make a beeline there.

She jumped into the reservoir.

She was in it for several moments, stunned senseless by the ice cold water, before she actually remembered diving in. Frantically, she tore open the snaps and buttons and zippers of her suit and put her hands inside, rummaging about, searching for the insect so she could pull the sucker out and drown it.

But she found nothing. When it came to her ambition for revenge, this was a disappointing development. How she had anticipated seeing it squirm as it tried to get away from her in the water! But on another level, she was tremendously relieved. Insanity she could deal with; physical pain was definitely a cause for panic.

Ariel imagined that perhaps the ant had been real after all, and had just torn through the suit on the way out. But the water around her, while not exactly clear, was very still.

There was no evidence of movement beneath the surface. Even the sand and dirt she'd raised upon entering had settled down by now.

She calmed herself with an effort, closed her eyes again, and waited.

Soon she felt reasonably assured that the insect wasn't real enough to attack her, but she stayed in the water just to be on the safe side. The water sent pinpricks of pain cascading through her very marrow—but even that kind of discomfort didn't provide her with enough incentive to get out.

Wolruf sat patiently on the bank. "Are 'u well again?" the alien asked.

"I think so," she said. "I had another visit."

"Assumed as much."

"I think my visitor is gone now. I think I prefer looking at my episodes in terms of visitors, by the way. It's making it easier for me to accept them."

"Good. Don't 'u wan' come out of water now? 'U mite catch cold."

"No. It feels rebellious, to be doing something prying robot eyes might disapprove of."

"Will wait."

"Thanks. I'll just be a few more minutes. However safe my mind may feel while I'm in here, I don't think my body can take much more of this cold."

Something brushed against her. She glanced down to see that something had stirred the dirt up. Something too big to be just an ant. Something that was real.

"What's that?" she exclaimed.

"Wha'zz what?" Wolruf inquired.

But Ariel could not bring herself to answer. Her teeth were clattering too much. Screwing up her courage—which she felt was in short supply these days—she gingerly ducked her head beneath the surface, keeping her eyes open in the frigid fluid with an effort.

A hunk of metal lay half buried in the bottom of the reservoir. The gentle currents had removed enough of the dirt covering it to begin moving it back to the shore. Its stiff hand brushed again against her leg.

Its hand?

Ariel accidentally inhaled a noseful of water. She shot up to the surface, sputtering.

"Air-eel?" asked Wolruf. "Wha' is it?"

"It's a robot—there's a robot down here!"

"Wha'zz it doing there?" asked the caninoid, running to the edge of the water.

"I don't know. I think it's dead!"

"Robotzz can't die!"

"Maybe this one can. It looks like Lucius!"

CHAPTER 5
UNLEARN OR ELSE

Just before dawn, Derec went to sleep wondering what it would feel like to know who he was.

He knew he would dream. He would remember his dream, as always. He often searched the imagery of his dreams for a clue to his identity, figuring that his subconscious was doubtlessly signaling him information about this most personal of all his problems.

Often he dreamed he was a robot. Collectively, those dreams were always similar. He might begin in the survival pod, or in the diagnostic hospital, or even in his sleeping quarters in the house he had had Robot City provide for himself and his friends. Often he would accidentally uncover the Key to Perihelion; he would open a console panel, or open a cabinet, or even find it in his life-suit, and he would always use it.

The destination invariably filled him with keen disappointment, or even despair, for it would always be another place where he had been during the last few weeks, subtly altered, more menacing perhaps, but always fresh in his memory. Never did he dream of a place he had been before he lost his memory. There would be an accident—he would fall down a chasm opening up beneath his feet, a worker robot would misfunction and slice him open, or something else equally disastrous would happen.

But he would feel no pain. There would be no blood. He would look on his injured body, and see his skeletal structure revealed by his wound.

But not his skeletal bone. And therein lay the serious rub.

For he would have no bones to break, no flesh to tear. His skin would be plastic and his skeleton would be metal. There would be blinking lights where his muscles should be, and wires instead of arteries.

And he would feel no pain, no life-and-death anxiety about the wound, only a calmly overwhelming urge to repair himself as quickly as possible.

At that point the dream always ended, with Derec waking up in a cold sweat, staring at his hand and wondering if it just wasn't programmed to tremble at irrational fears, fears that he had always been programmed to experience, at random intervals.

He always settled back to sleep with an effort, and though not a reflective man he would invariably wonder, just for a moment, if, after you got past the obvious, there really was any difference between feeling like a human and feeling like a robot.

Sometimes the same dream, or a close variation on it, would begin again.

Tonight, however, as he tossed and turned, the dream was somewhat different.

Not surprisingly, it began in the square.

It was night, and Derec was alone. There was not an entity in sight. And as he looked at the slightly taller, slightly more freakish versions of the buildings around the square, he doubted there was an entity in the city.

But something was missing. He sensed that though the square was deserted, it was even emptier than it should be.

Something else should be here. Circuit Breaker! Where was Circuit Breaker?

Derec looked down to see that the plasticrete was crawling up his feet, fastening him to the spot. There was the distinct sensation of his feet merging with the plasticrete, of the meta-cells beginning to function in harmony with his biological cells. Derec held down his growing sense of panic with an effort. He did not know which he feared more: the conclusion, or awakening before he learned what it might be.

In a matter of moments the meta-cells completely smothered Derec. So thoroughly had the metallic cells mingled with his own that he did not know where they ended and where his began.

Strangely, he felt himself to be wider, taller, more physically substantial in every respect. He could not see nor move, yet found he had no yen to do either. He had become Circuit Breaker itself, gathering in the energy of the starlight, transforming it, amplifying it, and casting it out. He was stronger, sturdier, and more solid than he had ever been before.

But he had also lost his mind. Suddenly he had gone from a someone to a no one. He didn't even miss his sense of identity. He couldn't understand why he had wanted his memory back in the first place. What good could thinking and knowledge do him, standing so strong and bulky against the atmospheric tides?

Derec awoke gradually; a profound feeling of mental displacement aggravated him during those moments in which his mind hovered in the regions between waking and sleeping. In fact, those moments stretched out for an uncommonly long time. Both his immediate future and immediate past seemed hopelessly out of reach.

But the future already beckoned. He realized that for the last several moments he had been listening to a loud pounding on the door. He recalled an appointment with annoyance. It was too bad. He half wished he could return to sleep. He could certainly use it.

Oh well, there's nothing I can do about it now.

He rubbed his eyes. "Hold on," he said. "I'll be right there!"

But the knocking continued unabated, growing progressively more insistent. Now Derec was really annoyed. The persistent knocking, if it came from a human, would be very impolite. But robots had no choice but to be polite, regardless of the circumstances. What kind of robot would be so

obviously predisposed toward the overkill of unnecessarily
persistent knocking?

Derec suddenly realized. *Oh no! I'd forgotten it was
Harry!*

Derec dressed hurriedly, opened the door and, sure
enough, Harry was standing at the threshold. "I assume I
have not been knocking too long," the robot said. "I have a
hundred questions to ask you."

"And I've got a few more than that to ask you," Derec
replied, motioning him inside, "but I'm afraid we've got a
limited amount of time today."

"So am I to assume that you are interviewing Lucius
later?" asked Harry. "Why chat with that genius when you
have me around?" Then: "Was that good? Was it humorous?"

Derec tried to hide his smile. He didn't want to encourage
the robot, which didn't need it anyway. "I think you'll both
prove equally important to my studies of what's been happening to robots on this planet. Did you bring your friends
along?"

"M334 and Benny? No. They are working on a project of
some sort together. I think they want its nature to be a surprise."

"And it probably will be," said Derec sarcastically, "if the
events of the last few days have been any indication."

"Forgive me in advance, but was that remark also an attempt at humor?"

"Not really, no."

"I see. You must understand it is often difficult for a
robot to understand what a human's tone of voice means,"
said Harry, again very politely.

Derec decided to take the question seriously. "It was a
casual observation, a commentary laced with what I pre-
sumed to be light-heartedness, an attitude which frequently
gives rise to humor."

"It sounded sarcastic, insofar as I can comprehend these
things."

"Did it, now? Maybe M334 should be here after all. Our

conversation last night was your first real contact with the human race, wasn't it?" asked Derec, punching up a cup of coffee from the dispenser.

"Yes, and an auspicious one it was, too."

"Whose tone is elusive now, Harry? How long have your pathways been consumed with the objective to achieve humor?"

"Since the replicating disaster that almost destroyed Robot City, from which you saved us, thank-you-very-much."

"And since then you've been pursuing your goal with the single-mindedness characteristic of robots?"

"How else?"

"How else, indeed. Hasn't it ever occurred to you that even humor has its time and place, that the average human being simply can't bear to be around someone who answers every query or makes every casual observation with a smart remark? It gets predictable after a while, and can cause an otherwise pleasant social situation to undergo rapid deterioration. Which is another way of saying that it gets boring. Dull. Mundane. Predictable."

"It fails to elicit the proper response."

"Robots can't laugh," said Derec cryptically, sipping his coffee. As bitter as bile, it was exactly what his nerves cried out for.

"I see you have deduced the basic conundrum in which I've found myself since I embarked on my little project."

"Believe me, it's obvious. But seriously, Harry, how would you react if you were walking down the street and a manhole suddenly opened up beneath you and you fell in?"

"What is a manhole? Is that some kind of sexual reference?"

"Ah, no, a manhole is an opening in the street, usually covered, through which someone can enter into a sewer or a boiler."

"Can you be certain there is nothing covertly sexual in those words? I have been diligently studying the craft of the double entendre, but there is much I have yet to grasp because all I know about human sexual matters is what material the central computer calls up for me."

"I must personally inspect that material as soon as possible. But to keep to the main subject, how would you feel if you fell down a manhole?"

Harry almost shrugged. "I would feel like going boom."

"Seriously."

"My logic circuits would inform me that the end was near and, knowing me, would close themselves down in an orderly fashion before I suffered the indignity of random disruption."

"I see. And how would you feel if you were walking down the street and saw me falling down a manhole?"

"Why, logically, that should be hysterical. Unless of course you went splat before I could fulfill the demands of the First Law."

"Hmmm. You see, in such an eventuality, you would identify with my loss of dignity and, were you human, would relieve your anxiety by laughing. Before you rescued me, that is. The question is: how can you relieve anxiety if you can't laugh?"

"Everyone can *agree* it's funny. That is how my comrades inform me when they believe I am on the beam."

"But a comic performing jokes in front of an audience of robots can't stop his act after each joke to ask everyone if he's on the right track."

"There are ways around that. It is customary in a formal situation for robots to nod their heads if they think something is funny. At least, that is what I am trying to convince them to do."

Derec finished his coffee in a gulp and immediately punched up a second cup. "I see you've given this some thought."

"One or two."

"Is that an attempt at irony?"

"No, at a joke."

"I think that for other robots to find your sense of humor worthwhile, you're going to have to think of angles that relieve their own robotic anxieties. I'm not exactly sure what those would be. You could make fun of their foibles. Or you could write and perform skits about a robot who's so literal-minded that he sometimes can't understand what's really going on around him. Some of Shakespeare's characters have that trait, and they're human, but it makes sense that a robot character would exaggerate things to ludicrous lengths."

"You mean a character who understands the letters of the words but not their shades of meaning."

"But the audience will. As robots, they will naturally have positronic anxieties concerning their own literal-minded traits relieved by identifying with him. He doesn't necessarily have to be sympathetic, even; he could have the kind of personality robots would love to hate, if they were capable of either emotion."

"What kind of anxieties do humans have?"

"It's difficult for me to say. I don't remember any humans. I've just read a few books. Many of Shakespeare's jokes, his puns, his slapstick, have a ribald, bawdy humor that strikes me as slightly off-color today, despite the gulf of the centuries between us. So I guess it's safe to say there's always been a certain amount of sexual anxiety in human beings, and one of the ways they relieve it—or learn how to deal with it—is through humor."

Harry nodded as if he understood what Derec was talking about. *Now, if I only felt the same,* Derec thought. *I'm strictly on shaky ground here.*

"In that case, you could explain an old Spacer joke to me that I have been trying to work into my act."

"Okay. . . . Your act!?"

"My act. Until now I have only told jokes to my personal acquaintances—comrades who understand what I am attempting to do. But I have been preparing a presentation for an assembly. An act."

"How many jokes do you have?"

"A couple. I have failed to generate original material, so I have been investigating the vocal rhythms behind existing jokes."

"To hone your timing?"

"Yes, insofar as I comprehend what that talent includes. There are no voice tapes for me to investigate, though the reference texts contain frequent entries on such material."

"Okay, Harry," said Derec, chuckling at the concept of all this as he folded his arms across his chest and leaned against the counter. "Fire away!"

"With post haste, sir. One day three men in a lifepod are coming in for a landing at the local spacedock. They had been marooned for several days and eagerly anticipate their return to the comforts of civilization. One man is a Settler, another an Auroran, and the third a Solarian."

Derec hid his grin with his palm. Harry's delivery was indeed awkward, and his few gestures bore little connection to what he was saying, but a solid effort was apparent. Also, the unlikely combination of the characters' derivations already promised interesting interaction. Historically, there was much social friction between the groups: Aurorans and Solarians both disliked the Settlers because of their recent "third-class" colonization of the planets; and there had never been much love lost between the Aurorans and Solarians, especially since the latter had mysteriously abandoned their world and vanished. Derec already made a mental note to tell Ariel this one.

"So the three men are just overhead the dock when suddenly a freighter's radar malfunctions and the gigantic ship crosses directly in front of their flight path. A crash is inevitable, and the three men prepare themselves for their last moments.

"A logical thing to do," said Derec. Immediately, he feared that his words might have disrupted Harry's rhythm, such as it was, and so resolved to remain quiet for the duration of the joke.

Harry, on the other hand, continued doggedly as if nothing had happened. "All of a sudden—mere instants before the crash—all three men are bathed in a yellow light—and they disappear into thin air!

"They look around and they fail to perceive their pod, the freighter, or the docks. They are in some kind of infinite pool of blue light—face-to-face with a strange man with a wreath of leafy twigs around his head. The strange man has a white beard, wears burlap robes, and carries a wooden staff. The men realize they are in the company of some kind of deity.

"'I am known throughout the spheres of space and time as He Who Points The Fickle Finger Of Fate,' the man says, 'and I have come to point the finger at you.' And true to his word, he points at the Settler and says, 'You shall live through the next few moments, but only if you promise never again to drink any sort of alcoholic beverage. Ever. The moment you take a drink, regardless of how many years from now it is, you will die an instant death. Do you understand?'

"'I do, sir,' says the Settler, 'though is it not asking much from a Settler to expect him to forego the delights of alcohol for an entire lifetime?'

"'Perhaps it is,' says He Who, 'but my demand stands nonetheless. I repeat, the instant a liquid containing alcohol touches your lips, you shall die as surely as if you had died in the crash.'

"'Then I agree,' says the Settler reluctantly.

"And He Who points to the Auroran and says, 'You must give up all greed.'

"'I accept!' says the Auroran at once. 'It's a deal!'

"And He Who points to the Solarian and says, 'And last, you must give up all sexual thoughts, except for those you might have strictly for purposes of socially acceptable wedded bliss.'

"'Excuse me, sir,' says the Solarian, 'but that is impossible. Do you not know what we Solarians have been through? Because our centuries of social and personal repression have ended so recently, we have little choice but to think about our new freedoms, and often.'

"He Who frowns and shakes his head. 'That is no concern of mine. The three of you have my terms. Accept them or die.'

"'I accept it,' the Solarian says.

"There is another flash of blinding light, and the three men find themselves standing on the ground as, in the distance, their pod crashes spectacularly into the freighter. They all experience profound relief. The Settler wipes his forehead and says, 'I am ecstatic that this little episode has concluded. Look, yonder is a bar. Join me as I down some spirits by way of celebrating our good fortune.'

"The Auroran and the Solarian agree. They both desire libation, and in addition desire to see what will happen to the Settler.

"Indeed, the very second that the Settler consumes his first drink, he dies on the proverbial spot. 'Leaping galaxies, the strange man was speaking the truth,' says the Auroran. 'We must vacate these premises!'

"The Solarian agrees enthusiastically. But on the way out the Auroran espies a rare and valuable jewel beneath a deserted table. The Auroran cannot resist. And just as he bends over to pick up the jewel—the Solarian dies!"

Harry ceased talking, and the longer Derec waited for the robot's next words, the more apparent it became that the joke was over. At first he didn't understand and he had to visualize the scene and what must have happened. The Auroran bending over . . . the Solarian breaking his word. . . .

Derec burst out laughing. "Ha, ha! That's pretty good. Very unpredictable."

"I understand that, sir," Harry said. "I realize that the narrative leads you to believe the Auroran is next, but I fail to comprehend exactly what the Solarian could possibly have been thinking of. The central computer has thus far been unable to find material that would enlighten me. Would you care to explain?"

"No, no. I really do believe there are some things a robot was not meant to know."

"Do I have your permission to ask Miss Ariel the same question?"

"Not before I ask her something slightly similar." He took Harry by the arm and began leading him toward the door. "Now I've got to get you out of here. Lucius is due, and I'd like to talk to him alone, if you don't mind."

"Sir, how could I possibly do that?" Harry asked.

"Just a figure of speech," said Derec, reaching for the doorknob. But before he had a chance to touch it, the door opened from the other side.

Ariel, her hair dripping wet and her suit clinging to her body, came running into the house. "There you are!" she exclaimed.

"Don't you ever knock?" Derec asked angrily, then calmed down when he realized something serious was the matter. Besides, of course she didn't have to knock. She lived here, too. "Are you all right?"

"Yes, of course. Wolruf and I found, ah. . . ."

"Well? Out with it!" exclaimed Derec.

"I was at the reservoir this morning," she said haltingly. "Uh, I was *in* the reservoir, and I felt something strange. It was Lucius. His positronic brain had been partially destroyed."

"What did you say?" asked Derec as the room began to spin.

"Lucius has been deliberately sabotaged. To the utmost degree. You might even say he's been murdered."

"Ridiculous," said Harry calmly. "Only an outsider would have committed such a deed, and that's impossible. The city would have responded to an alien presence."

"Not necessarily," said Derec, thinking of Doctor Avery, who kept an office here, and whose arrival surely would not activate the city's automatic warning devices.

"It's no accident," said Ariel firmly. "I think you'll agree. Wolruf is supervising the robots who are bringing the, ah, body over here. Then you'll both see for yourselves."

"One of you must know more," said Harry. "A robot would not willingly harm another robot. Only you two and the alien are suspects."

Derec rubbed his chin thoughtfully. "No, there is no law actually dictating that a robot shall not do violence to another robot. In fact, a robot would have no choice if he truly believed harm would come to a human as a result of his omission of action." He glanced at Ariel. "Where's Mandelbrot? Wolruf?"

"Supervising the robots carrying the body here," she said.

"Harry, please leave immediately. We'll finish our talk later."

"All right," said the robot, walking through the door. "Though I feel obligated to warn you: You have not perceived my presence for the last time!"

"Is that robot for real?" asked Ariel after it was gone.

"I'm afraid so," Derec replied. "Are you certain that we're dealing with a deliberate case of deactivation here— not an accident of some sort?"

"No—but, Derec, Lucius's face was struck in several places. It certainly looked deliberate to me, as if someone wanted to ensure it couldn't be identified."

"Which is impossible, because most of its parts contain serial numbers, which can be traced."

"Exactly. So whoever did it must have realized that in mid-act and then thrown Lucius in the reservoir in the hope that it wouldn't be found. Or, if it was found, it'd be so rusty that most of the serial numbers would be obscured."

"And unless we've an unidentified intruder—which seems unlikely—a robot was responsible."

"Amazing, isn't it?"

Derec nodded. "Absolutely. What were you doing in the reservoir?"

Ariel blushed, though Derec couldn't tell if it was from anger or embarrassment. "I was taking a swim."

"Fully dressed? Say, you've been losing weight, haven't you?" he asked, looking her over with wide eyes.

"You'll never know. Derec, how can you be flip at a time like this? To lose Lucius—"

"So early in his career, I know. The galaxy has been

robbed of a great artist, I fear. Tragic. Simply tragic. I have to laugh, Ariel. It's the only way I can deal with it, and right now I don't care if you understand or not! Now be quiet and let me think!''

Ariel blinked in surprise, and jerked her head back as if he had taken a swipe at her. But she did as he wished.

Derec stared at the wall and tried to remember when he and Mandelbrot had parted company with Lucius. There had been a few hours remaining until the dawn. Had Lucius said anything about where it was going or what it was going to do? Nothing in particular that Derec could recall, just that it was going to close down for a few hours before beginning work on its next project. No, there wouldn't be any clues; Lucius certainly couldn't have predicted or even suspected that it would be murdered.

Hmm, can you call the shutdown of a robot "murder"? Derec asked himself. *Or is murder too strong a word to use when talking about a machine, regardless of its level of sophistication?*

A few moments later, however, Derec realized he wasn't ruminating on the incident so much as he was repressing a profound sense of outrage. During their few hours together, Lucius had begun to mean something special to him. True, there was the possibility that he was overreacting because of his already well established affinity for robots, but throughout his short life that he could remember, he had demonstrated a special appreciation for intelligent life in all its manifestations.

Lucius was a robot, Derec thought. *But I fear I shall never see its like again.*

Derec realized after the fact that he had paraphrased a line from Shakespeare's *Hamlet*. This reminded him of the promise he had made to Lucius, and he mulled over the implications of this promise for long minutes after Mandelbrot and Wolruf had escorted the robots carrying Lucius inside, after they had lain Lucius on a table. Evidently Mandelbrot or Ariel must have ordered the robots to depart, because Derec never recalled giving such an order.

For a while, as he looked at the battered and distorted face, Derec hoped he would discover that it was a dreadful mistake, that it really wasn't Lucius there after all, but some other robot. But the size was right. The model was right. The color was right. The unique identifying features that all city robots possessed to some degree were right. But most of all, the feeling in Derec's gut was right.

Lucius was indeed dead. Murdered. The logic circuits of its positronic brain had been removed with precision. But the personality integrals had been left in the brain cavity, left to be permanently damaged in the reservoir. So Lucius's unique abilities at logic might still exist, but the interaction between brain and body would probably never again be achieved. The personality was gone forever.

"Excuse me, everyone," Derec said, actually aware that his friends were staring at him, waiting for his reaction. "I'd like to be alone with Lucius for a few moments."

And then, after they had left, Derec cried. He cried in pity and remorse, not for Lucius, but for himself. This was the first time he could remember having cried. When he finished, he felt only marginally better, but he had some idea of what he had to do, and who to look to for an answer.

Derec found the ebony at the place he had come to think of as Circuit Breaker Square. Other robots of various models and intelligence levels stood around the building, watching its colors reflect the sunlight in muted shades. Occasionally, reflections thrown off by the smooth planes glittered against the robots and the other buildings. The overall effect of Circuit Breaker was more restrained in the sunlight. Doubtlessly that, too, had been part of Lucius's plan, to permit the building to become controllable and hence "safer" in the day, while the night unleashed its true energies. He would have to find out upon what principle the solar batteries worked.

That was another question Lucius would no longer be

able to answer personally; however interesting it was on the purely scientific level, it did not seem especially important in light of recent events.

The ebony stood at the edge of the perimeter. Its head never turned to the building; it was watching the other robots instead, as if it was searching for some meaning in their activity. Or lack of it, as the case was. The ebony stood straight and tall, with barely a nuance Derec could call remotely human. It was easy for him to imagine a black cape hanging from the ebony's shoulders, easier still to imagine it standing on a hilltop and glaring in defiance at a gathering storm.

Blow wind, and crack your cheeks, Derec thought, recalling a line from *King Lear.*

Trying his best to look casual, as if he were simply taking a stroll, Derec walked to the ebony and said, "Excuse me, but didn't I see you here last night?"

"It is possible, master," replied the ebony, bowing its head and shoulders slightly as if to take note of the human's presence for the first time.

"With all the other robots?"

"I was in the square, but my circuits do not acknowledge the fact that I was *with* the other robots."

"I see by your insignia and model that you are a supervisor robot."

"That is true."

"Exactly what are your duties?" Derec asked casually.

With an almost stately turn of its head, the ebony turned toward Circuit Breaker and waited until the length of the silence between them became quite long—deliberately, for a kind of dramatic effect, it seemed to Derec. An answer was intended, but so was a space of waiting. Derec began to get a seriously queasy feeling in his stomach.

Finally, the ebony said, "My duties are floating. I am programmed to ascertain what needs to be done and then to do it or otherwise see to it."

"All of this is up to your discretion?"

"I am a duly designated rogue operative. The city requires a certain amount of random checks if it is to run at peak efficiency. If a machine breaks down gradually, the supervisor on the spot might not notice because it is there during every tour of duty. It would get used to the situation, would not even realize something was amiss, whereas I, with my extra-keen memory banks and an eye capable of perceiving individual levels of meta-cells, would notice it immediately."

"Once you actually look at the problem, that is."

"Of course. I doubt even a human can fix a machine before he knows if and where it has been broken."

"Don't underestimate us."

"I shall strive not to. Do not think, sir, that my sole function is to act as mechanical troubleshooter. My tasks vary, depending upon the situation. Often central calls on me to provide visual and cognitive assistance if there is some problem with robotic efficiency—not that my comrades ever function at less than their peak, but because sometimes they cannot be certain that they are directing their energies to the best advantage of all."

"So you're a problem solver! You help devise solutions to the unforeseen shortcomings in central's program!"

Derec leaned against a building and saw Circuit Breaker weave back and forth like a balloon hung up in a breeze. He felt like someone had hit him on the back of the skull with a lug wrench. His lungs felt like paper. His ankles felt like the bones had turned into rubber putty. At first he was too stunned to loathe the ebony, but that feeling grew and grew, as he leaned there and tried to get his thoughts straight.

This robot has got to make decisions, Derec thought. *The very nature of its job calls for analytical creativity! It could have viewed Circuit Breaker as so revolutionary to the robotic psyche that it constituted an obstacle to the laborers' duties. And then . . . then the ebony would have been forced to do something about Lucius.*

There's nothing in the Three Laws about a robot being

forbidden to harm another robot. In fact, First Law situations and Second Law orders may require it.

This is not proof, though.

For a moment Derec wondered what he would do once he had the proof. He would have to keep the ebony—or whichever robot the murderer was—functional for a time until the mechanics as well as the psychology had been checked for anomalies. The question of what came next would have to be decided after all the facts were in. It was possible that the ebony couldn't help itself.

Just as it was also possible that the Three Laws had been a significant factor, that once the ebony had embarked on a course of logic, it had followed it rigorously to an end predestined for tragedy.

"Tell me," Derec said, making an effort to stand up straight, "do you ever take the initiative when it comes to identifying problems?"

"If you mean can I pinpoint a potential glitch before central is aware, then the answer is yes. Those occasions, however, are quite rare and often quite obvious."

"They're obvious if you're not central."

"Sir?"

"And do you ever take the initiative in solving problems?"

"I have, and central has had to fine-tune them, too."

"But not all the time."

"I see I must be exact about this. Central has only fine-tuned three out of forty-seven of my solutions. Have I satisfied you so far with my answers, sir?"

"Forty-seven? That's a lot of problems, and those are only the ones you found on your own."

"Robot City is young, sir. There will doubtlessly be many glitches in the system before the city is operating at one hundred percent efficiency."

"And you're certainly going to do your bit, aren't you?"

"I can do nothing else, sir."

Derec nodded. "I see. By the way, what's your name?"

"Canute."

"Tell me, Canute, how would you rate—efficiency-wise —a robot that deliberately took it upon itself to disconnect a comrade?"

"Sir, it would have to be seriously examined. Though of course it is possible that the First or Second Law would permit such an action."

"Are you aware that someone, presumably a robot, brutally disconnected Lucius last night? Damaged him beyond all hope of repair?"

"Of course I am aware. News travels fast over the comlink."

"So you heard about it from other robots first?"

"Sir, why not ask me outright if I was the robot responsible? You know I am forbidden to lie."

Canute's words were like a bucket of cold water thrown into Derec's face. Their forthrightness startled him. "I—I— how did you know I was leading up to that?"

"It seemed obvious from your line of questioning."

"I see you have advanced deductive abilities."

"It is a prerequisite for my line of work."

Hmmm. I think you just may be the kind of robot I need, Derec thought. Putting aside his feelings for Lucius with a force of will, he thought of Ariel, and of the possibility that Canute, who made its intuitive leaps from a solidly practical framework, would be just the one to help him diagnose and cure her disease. Once its mental frames of reference could be adjusted, that is.

The trick would be to get it to readjust—to admit the gravity of its error—without causing positronic burnout in the process. For in that eventuality, Canute wouldn't be able to repair a paper clip.

So the direct approach was out. Besides, Derec had a promise to keep.

"Canute, you may find this hard to believe, but I've been looking for a model like you."

"Sir?"

"Yes, I have a specific type of building in mind that I'd like to see erected nearby. I'd also like it as permanent as possible. I think its presence will do much to enrich life here in Robot City."

"Then I am eager to do whatever you ask. What type of building did you have in mind?"

"An open-air theatre—a playhouse. I'll give you the details later, but I want to see functional elaboration in the design. I want you to generate your notions of some of the details. In fact, I insist on it. Understand?"

"Yes," said Canute, lowering its head slightly. "May I ask why you want to have a theatre erected?"

"Have you ever heard of *Hamlet?*"

Canute was right about one thing: news travels fast at comlink speed. Returning from Circuit Breaker Square to his quarters, Derec hadn't even gotten through the door before Mandelbrot began talking.

"Master, where have you been? I have been besieged by requests to assist you in your latest project. I fear that, lacking sufficient information, I was forced to tell everyone to wait. I hope that was all right."

"It was," said Derec, lying down on the couch. "Where's Ariel?"

"She went to her room. She mumbled something about mopping up on her Shakespeare."

"I think you mean brushing up."

"If you say so."

"You're not very comfortable with human idioms, are you, Mandelbrot?"

"I can be neither comfortable nor uncomfortable conversing with them. But I take you to mean it is sometimes difficult for me to translate their peculiar surface meanings in practical terms. For instance, how do you brush up someone who is ancient history? In that respect, I do sometimes have problems communicating. But about this project. . . ."

"All right, I'll tell you. But wait—where's Wolruf?"

"With Miss Ariel. I think Wolruf is performing some task. Forgive me if I am again misphrasing it, but she is being Miss Ariel's line coach."

"Ssh. Quiet. Listen."

And Derec heard, very softly, through the closed door,

Ariel speaking the words, "Oh, what a noble mind is here o'erthrown! The courtier's, soldier's, scholar's, eye, tongue, sword; the expectancy and rose of the fair state, the glass of fashion and the mould of form, the observed of all observers, is, er, ah—"

"Kwei-it," said Wolruf in a low volume that wasn't hushed enough to be called a whisper, but was probably as close to one as she could manage.

"Quite, quite down!" Ariel finished enthusiastically.

"Hmm, it seems my second bit of casting is almost complete," said Derec.

"Casting, master?" said Mandelbrot. "You are having a cast made? Have you injured yourself?"

"No, not at all," Derec replied, laughing.

"I must say, it seemed you were hiding your suffering awfully well."

"It's my hobby. Listen, tell me what you would do with the robot that dismantled Lucius." The sudden shock of the image of the robot lying there, behind the closed door to his office, sent a tremor of loss and grief through Derec's veins. And of terror, too. He'd never before thought robots were things that could die. He'd always assumed they were immortal in a way that life could never be.

"Forgive me, master, but I would think nothing of it. I would merely follow your instructions."

"And what if I wasn't around to give you instructions? What if you had to decide when you were on your own?"

"First, I would solicit the robot's explanation, and learn of any justifications for its actions, if any, it may have had, particularly as they involved its interpretation of the Three Laws."

"But there is no law against a robot harming another robot."

"Of course, and the robot in question may have been operating on instructions from a human. But I gather such is not the case here."

"Well, yes . . ."

"So after having received the explanation, I would take

the safest course and have the robot closed down until the proper repairs could be administered, or until instructions could be received from human sources."

"That could take a long time, particularly here on Robot City."

"No harm would be done. Upon reactivation, if that is what is decided upon, the robot would behave as if it had just been shut down for a tune-up the day before."

"Hmm. But what if there was something you needed from the robot?"

"Then that would depend on what you needed, and how badly you needed it."

"I'm glad you feel that way, not that you can feel, I know, but it makes me feel better to know your logic circuits concur with some of this . . ." And he explained to Mandelbrot his theory that a creative robot with a scientific bent might be able to make a diagnostic breakthrough to help Ariel.

"But how do you know that Canute possesses scientific talents?"

"I don't. But I may be able to use its mind to help me learn more about what's happening to the robots in this place. And I need to do it—to get Canute to admit to its error without drifting out in the process. That's one reason why I'm putting on this play."

"This play?"

"*Hamlet*, by William Shakespeare. Quiet; listen."

Ariel's voice came through the door, muffled but quite clear as she repeated and then continued the speech she had rehearsed earlier, this time in louder, more confident cadences. "And I of ladies most deject and wretched, that suck'd the honey of his music vows, now see that noble and most sovereign reason, like sweet bells jangled, out of tune and harsh."

"Isn't that beautiful?" Derec gushed.

"The words, master, or Miss Ariel saying them?"

"Have you been talking to Harry?"

"Master, I do not understand your implication."

"Never mind. Anyway, I'm going to use this play as a

lightning rod, to draw every robot with creative tendencies to the same place, working on a group project, and then see what develops. I don't know what's going on here, but whatever it is, I'm going to bust it wide open!"

Someone knocked on the door. "Get that, will you?" Derec asked as he turned toward Ariel's office. "Ariel? This is your director speaking! Come out here, will you?"

Ariel came out in a flash, followed by a bounding Wolruf. "Director?" she said. "Then who's going to be my leading man?"

"Oh? When you found out about this production, how did you know you were going to be Ophelia?"

"Because clearly I possess all the mental and physical qualifications. Who better to play a girl who's going insane than one who really is? Of course, I don't know who's going to play Hamlet's mother, but that's not my problem, is it?"

At least she's keeping her sense of humor about things, Derec thought. "No—it's your director's—and your leading man's.".

Ariel grinned and bowed. "At your service, Mr. Director."

"Master—"

"Yes, Mandelbrot."

"Forgive the intrusion, Master Derec and Mistress Ariel, but Harry, Benny, and M334 are at the door. They said they had vibes to present to you."

"Vibess?" said Wolruf. "Not ni-ice word on my worrld."

"Yes, but who knows what it means here," said Ariel. "Send them in, Mandelbrot."

"Yes, I suppose we have to begin interviewing for our cast and crew sooner than later," said Derec.

In walked the three robots, each carrying brass objects. Each object struck Derec as being rather strange. M334 held a tube with two dozen keys, with what appeared to be a mouthpiece on one end. It was evidently a wind instrument, though what sort of sound it was supposed to make, Derec had no way of imagining.

Nor did he know what sort of sounds he might expect from the other two instruments held by the other two robots. Benny's was smaller than M334's, and could be easily held in one hand; there were three taps on the top, presumably to modulate the sonic textures. Harry's was the straightest and the longest of the three; it had a sliding device that evidently would lengthen or shorten the tubing to match the player's will, again presumably to modulate the sound.

"Good day, sir," said Benny. "We can only presume we are interrupting your preparations—"

"Good grief, word travels fast around here!" Ariel exclaimed.

"*You* found out, didn't you?" said Derec.

Ariel shrugged. "I heard it from Wolruf."

"And how did you hear about it, Wolruf?" Derec asked.

Wolruf merely shrugged. The effort made her entire body quiver.

"—And so we thought you might want to see for yourself the results of a project we have been devoting ourselves to instead of closing down in our spare time," finished Benny, as if no one else had spoken.

"Ah, and what is the nature of this project?" Derec asked suspiciously.

"Originally it was purely musical," said Benny.

"But when we heard you were planning to engage us in a recreation of human art forms, we performed research and discovered that music was often a significant part of such functions," said Harry.

"That struck us as being particularly fortuitous," said M334. "We thought—perhaps presumptuously, but how could we tell if we refrained from inquiring?—that our music might make a significant contribution to the enterprise."

"Uh, what kind of music are we attempting here, with those things?" Ariel asked. "Auroran nouveau fugues? Tantorian ecto-variations?"

"Something close to period, Terran-style," said Harry.

"You mean from Earth?" Ariel asked incredulously. Terran culture was not held in high regard in most Spacer circles.

"Shakespeare was from Earth," put in Derec mildly.

"Yes, but he was lucky enough to be talented," said Ariel. "You can't say that about most Terran artists."

"Perhaps you judge our aspirations too harshly," said Benny.

"Yes, you should judge after you hear us play," said M334.

"Yes, you should have plenty of critical ammunition then," said Harry.

Ariel stared at Derec. "It was a joke," Derec said.

"Close to bein' good one!" said Wolruf.

The three robots then magnetically applied computerized, flexible, artificial lips to their speaker grills. The lips were connected by electrical cords that led into the positronic cavities, and Derec saw at once, by the way the robots exercised the lips and blew air through them, that they responded directly to thought control.

Just like real lips, thought Derec, biting his lower one as if to make sure. "Excuse me, but before you boys strike up the brass, I'd like to know what names those instruments are supposed to have."

"This is a trumpet," said Benny.

"A saxophone," said M334.

"And a trombone," said Harry.

"And by way of further introduction," said Benny, "the number we would like to assault for your aural perusal is an ancient composition dating not four hundred years later than Shakespeare's time. This was already during the age of recorded music, but no tapes are currently available through central, so we can only surmise the manner in which these instruments were played by examining the sheet music."

"What there is of it," said Harry. "Most of this number is improvised."

"Uh-oh!" said Ariel to herself, putting her hand protectively on her forehead. *"I must be having a delirium!"*

"And the number we would like to assault is what the reference tapes denote as, in the parlance of the day, a snappy little ditty. This song its composer, the human known as Duke Ellington, called 'Bouncing Buoyancy.'"

I've got a bad feeling about this, Derec thought. He waved his hand. "Play on, McDuffs!"

The robots did. At least, that's what the humans and the alien thought they were trying to do. The musical form was so radically unlike anything they'd experienced, the playing so haphazard and odd, so full of accidental spurts and sputters and stops, that exactly what the robots were attempting to do remained a matter of some conjecture.

Benny's trumpet played the lead with a blaring succession of notes that occasionally struck the ear as being just right. The noise the instrument made resembled the wail of a siren, recorded backwards. So high was its frequency that Derec became afraid his ears would begin bleeding. Benny's notes, on the other hand, did seem to possess some kind of internal logic, as if he knew where he was going but wasn't quite sure how to get there.

Harry on the trombone and M334 on the saxophone attempted to provide Benny with a solid foundation; awkwardly, they tooted eight measures of unchanging harmony, over and over again. They nearly succeeded, harmony-wise, and perhaps their glitches wouldn't have been so noticeable if they'd occasionally managed to start and end the eight measures at the same time.

The trombone itself tended to sound like an exquisitely crafted raspberry, surreally brayed from the mouth of a contemptuous donkey. The saxophone's sonic attack, meanwhile, resembled nothing so much as a gaggle of geese gurgling underwater. The effect of the three instruments combined was such that Derec wondered momentarily if the robot hadn't come up with a violation of an interplanetary weapons treaty.

Derec spent the first minute finding the music absolutely atrocious, utterly without redeeming social value. It was the worse kind of noise; that is, noise pretending to be something else. But gradually he began to perceive, vaguely, the equally vague ideal in the robots' minds. The music itself, regardless of the manner of its playing, possessed a single-minded joy that quickly became infectious. Derec discovered that his toe was tapping in a rhythm akin to that of the music. Ariel was nodding thoughtfully. Wolruf had her head cocked inquisitively, and Mandelbrot was his usual inscrutable self.

Derec's mind wandered a second, and he wondered if he could rig up a specimen of those liplike fixtures on the mouths to help robots portray human emotions during the production. The fact that most had immobile faces, incapable of even rudimentary expression, was going to cripple the illusion unless he devised some way to use the very inflexibility to greater effect. He imagined a set of lips twisted in laughter at the play's cavorting actors, and in fear of the ghost of Hamlet's father, and in anguish at the sight of all the dead bodies littering the stage. *Well, it's a thought,* he figured, and then returned his attention to the music.

The arrangement of "Bouncing Bouyancy" concluded with all three instruments playing the main theme simultaneously. Theoretically. The robots took the mouthpieces from their lips with a flourish and held out the instruments toward their audience.

Derec and Ariel looked at one another. Her expression read *You're the director, you do the talking*.

"How did our number bludgeon you, master?" asked Benny.

"Uh, it was certainly unusual. I think I see what you robots are trying to get at, and I think I may like it if you actually get there. Don't you agree, Ariel?"

"Oh, yes, definitely." She was really saying *I seriously doubt it*.

"Iss it *Ham-lit?*" Wolruf asked.

"That, I don't know," said Derec. "I suppose this Ellington fellow composed other works, though."

"In a variety of styles and moods," said Benny.

"All adaptable to our instruments," said Harry.

"I was afraid of that," Derec said. "But don't worry. I'm sure you'll improve with practice. I take it this has been your secret project, Benny?"

Benny bowed in a manner curiously appreciative for a robot. "I personally crafted the instruments and taught my friends what knowledge I had concerning the art of blowing horns."

"Take off those lips, will you? They're just too weird."

As the robots complied, Mandelbrot said, "Master, this performance. Where will it take place? I do not believe the city has theatrical facilities."

"Don't worry. I've got it taken care of. I know just the robot who can design us a theatre perfectly suited for the denizens of Robot City. Only he doesn't know about it yet."

"And who is that, master?"

"Canute. Who else?" Derec smiled. "In fact, get me Canute. Have him come here right away. I want him to hear some of this 'Bouncing Bouyancy' brew."

"Each age has different terrors and tensions," said Derec a few days later on the stage of the New Globe, "but they all open on the same abyss."

He paused to see what effect his words had on the robots sitting in the chairs before the proscenium. He had thought his words exceedingly profound, but the robots merely stared back at him as though he had recounted the symbols of a meaningless equation, interesting only because a human had happened to say it.

He cleared his throat. Sitting in seats off to the side of the robots were Ariel and Mandelbrot. Ariel had a notebook in hand, but Mandelbrot, whom Derec had appointed property master, naturally had no need of one; his total recall would keep track of the production's prop specifications without notes.

Wolruf sat licking her paw in a chair just behind the pair. She had insisted on being the official prompter, or line coach, and as such had already spent a lot of time prompting Derec and Ariel while they were memorizing their lines—a task that he feared, in his own case, was far from completed.

Derec cleared his throat again. His awkwardness showed —at least if the knowing smile Ariel directed toward him was any indication. Wolruf just licked her chops; he got the feeling that on an unspoken level, she was finding the shenanigans of humans and robots incredibly amusing.

"Hmmm. You're all familiar with the studies some of you have been making concerning the Laws of Humanics. That means you're also familiar, at least in passing, with the many peculiarities and contradictions of the human condition. Passion and madness, obsession and nihilism—these things don't exist among you robots, but it's something we humans have to deal with, in varying degrees, every day.

"Shortly, we shall boldly go where no robot has gone before. We shall descend into the dense, dark, deep, decrepit abyss of the thirst for revenge, and when we emerge, we'll have something—something—something *really* terrific to remember in the days ahead. It'll be swell. You'll see."

"Get on with it!" Ariel shouted.

"Forgive me, master, but it is my considered opinion that you should get on to the more theatrical matters," piped in Mandelbrot. In an effort to appear natural, he had crossed his legs and held his palms on his knee. He succeeded only in appearing like a bunch of plywood pounded together with rusty nails.

"It's all right, Mandelbrot," said Derec, feeling his face flush. "I'm just getting warmed up." Returning his attention to the robots, he could not fail to notice their posture was every bit as stiff as his robot Friday's. For a brief instant, he wondered *What in the world am I doing here?*, steeled himself, and promptly got on with it. "Theatre is an art that depends upon the work of many collaborators—" he began.

Here was the New Globe Theatre, designed by the robot Canute and built under its personal supervision. By following the leads of clues in the central computer that Lucius had left when it had used its programs, Canute was able to tell the city what to build and how long it should stand. Meaning that Canute had done pretty much what Lucius had done, but acting under orders from a human. (While supervising this aspect of his project, Derec realized it was possible that Lucius had, in turn, followed leads suggested by Derec's establishment of automats in one building out of every ten. But of course Derec would never know for certain.)

Perhaps the task has been easier, less taxing for Canute because, unlike Lucius, he had had a pattern to follow: that of the old Globe Theatre in the London, Earth, of Shakespeare's day. But he had added his own specifications, without Derec's prompting. He had attempted to ascertain the special problems of form and function and how they either augmented or conflicted with his sense of how a theatre should fit in esthetically with the environment of Robot City.

Derec had pointedly refrained from telling Canute why the ebony, of all the robots in the city, had been appointed to design the second permanent building of Robot City. And he had watched Canute carefully while giving instructions, to see if it was in danger of positronic drift for doing (Derec suspected) exactly what it had harmed another robot for doing.

But Canute had given no such evidence. All that was needed to satisfy it, apparently, was for the impetus to come from human instructions.

Like the old Globe, Canute's theatre was roughly cylindrical in shape, but it was also misshapen and bent, like a bar of metal that had been slightly melted on the ground, then twisted beneath a giant foot. Like the old Globe—or at least according to most of the conjectures that had been made about it after it had been torn down to make room for a row of tenements a few decades after Shakespeare's death—there were three trap doors in the stage, leading to different areas backstage. One backstage passage led as well to the city's underground conduits, in case there was a power problem.

There were both a gallery and an upper gallery above the stage, and several hidden cameras in the wings. The rows of seats were staggered to provide each patron with an unobstructed view of the proceedings. Continuing the effort of providing the audience with the best possible lines of sight, the floor was raised and leveled in a series of gradual steps.

And, in the tradition of modern concert venues, tremendous screens for close-up shots were hung above the stage. Microphones were concealed throughout the stage and galleries.

Even the size of the theatre was impressive. The angles of the design provided for a variety of possible dramatic effects. But it was Canute's choice of colors that really made the New Globe something to shout about over the hyperwave. On the jet-black ceiling, sparkles wavered in and out of focus like stars seen through a haze of heat. The carpet and seats were in gray-brown tones, variations of the colors found in the conduits and on the surface of the city—Canute's version of "earth-tones." The curtain was a flaming crimson that sparkled, too, and the walls were a soft, demure shade of white. The soft currents of the air conditioning system continuously rippled the curtains.

Robots naturally had no need of air conditioning, giving Derec the impression that Canute had designed the theatre not only for robots, but for humans as well. As if the ebony had designed the theatre in the secret, perhaps unrecognized hope that one day a play for an audience of humans would be presented here.

The subconscious hope?

"As robots, you are constitutionally incapable of telling a lie," Derec said to his unresponsive audience. "Only human beings can do that, though not always successfully. Theatre, however, is a world of pretense, provoking the collaborative activity of the spectator's imagination. The spectator must be ready, willing, and able to believe in the lie of fiction, in the hopes of finding amusement, and, perhaps, some enlightenment. Our job is to assist him, to make him want to believe the lie.

"On the Shakespearean stage, little was shown, but everything was signified. Speech, action, prop, setting—all worked together toward the common end of providing the viewer a window through which he could look on the world.

And if all the efforts of the cast and crew were successful, then the viewer, knowing that what he was seeing was a fabrication, *willingly suspended his disbelief,* choosing to believe for the moment that what he was seeing was real for the purpose of relating to the story.

"Our challenge is different. We must aid, force, and agitate robots to exercise their logic integrals in such a way that the integrals, too, become suspended. We must not only provide a window to the world, but to the heart of Man.

"As I understand it, there are three worlds which must be considered for every production. That's the world of the play, the world of the playwright, and the world of the production. I think we can all agree on what the world of the production is; I'd like to say a few words about the other two worlds."

"Are you going to perform this play—or talk it to death?" Ariel called out mischievously.

Derec laughed nervously. She had thrown him off his rhythm, and he forgot what he had planned to say next.

"The world of the playwright," Mandelbrot prompted helpfully.

"Okay. In our time, mankind has achieved, more or less, an utterly civilized life. Few men ever break the laws of Man. Most people live long, healthy lives, even on overpopulated Earth, where conditions aren't too terrific.

"But in Shakespeare's day, life was often less a gift to be savored than it was a bagatelle to be endured. Working conditions were brutal and difficult, education was nonexistent except for the privileged classes, and the scientific way of thinking—based on logical thinking with empirical proof backing it up—was only beginning its ascendancy. Most people died before they were thirty-five, thanks to war, pestilence, persecution, lousy hygiene, things of that nature. After all, Queen Elizabeth I of England, the ruler of Shakespeare's day, was considered odd because she took a bath once a month, whether she needed it or not. But—yes, what is it?" Derec asked, noting that a robot sitting near Canute in the front had tentatively raised its hand.

"Most humble, abject, piteous apologies tendered for this untimely interruption," said the robot, "but after having read the text and pondered its meanings for several hours, I find myself unhappily fixated on a problem of overwhelming significance, and it's reasonable for me to trust that only a human being can explain it adequately."

"Of course. I welcome any question."

"Even one of a subjective nature?"

"Naturally."

"Even one that may in some quarters be considered too impolite for normal social intercourse?"

"Of course. Shakespeare was a missionary in opening up the realms of Terran discussion for centuries."

"Even if the question is personal?"

Without trying to be obvious about it, Derec glanced down at his crotch to see if his zipper was up. "Why, uh, sure. We're going to have some pretty complex motivations in basic human drives to examine here."

"Even if the question may be *extremely* personal?"

"What?"

"Is that a direct order?"

"No, it's a direct question, but you can take it as an order if only it will get you to come out with it!"

"Excellent. For a moment I was afraid my capacitors would not permit me utterance if I was not bouyed by the added impetus of a direct order."

"Would you please tell me what's on your mind?"

"I know that the human male and female tend to have different surface contours, and that this difference has something to do with their frequently complex social interaction, and so my question is simply this: just what is it that the human male and female seem to be doing to each other in all their spare time?"

A stony silence echoed throughout the theatre. Derec's focus wavered, and the gentle hum of the air conditioning went through a progression of hypnotic wah-wahs, as if it had been filtered in a recording studio. He shot Ariel a questioning glance. She smiled and shrugged. He looked at Wolruf.

She shook her head. "Don' look a' me. We have no matin' cuss'oms. Jus' do it and done be."

"I seriously doubt it," Derec snapped back. He happened to glance stage left just as Harry, holding the trombone, stuck its head from the wings. Benny and M334, also holding their instruments, stood behind Harry and gestured as if to grab the robot by the shoulders and pull it back.

They evidently thought better of it though, and permitted Harry to say, "Mister Director, I believe I can shake some illumination on the situation."

Derec bowed, and gestured him onto the stage. "Be my guest."

But as Harry quickly walked out and stood before the audience of robots, Derec suddenly got a sinking sensation in his stomach. "Uh, Harry, this isn't another one of your jokes, is it?"

"I believe it shall prove instructive."

"All right. I know when I'm beat." Derec moved away to stand between Ariel and Wolruf.

Harry did not even look at the humans before commencing. He concentrated his gaze on the robots. "An axiom of carbon-based life-forms is that nature has intended them to reproduce. Not necessarily on schedule, not necessarily when it's convenient, not necessarily prettily, but well. If the life-form in question derives a certain amount of gratification in the act of reproducing, that is well and good as far as the life-form is concerned, but all nature cares about is the reproductive urge. Some visual data is available from central, and I suggest you study it at your leisure, so we can all understand what chemical reactions are driving Ophelia and Hamlet while the latter is putting aside the pleasures of the moment to gain his crown." Harry nodded at Derec. "You see, I have read the play already." Then, back to the audience:

"And so that you might understand the dark, innermost

depths of the urge, I must direct your attention to the early days of mankind's colonization of the planets, in the days before he had truly accepted robots as his faithful companions, in the days when the wars of Earth, with their nuclear missiles and space-based defense systems, had followed man to the stars. In those days, military bases on newly colonized planets were common, and generally they were positioned at points remote from the civilian installations.

"And, in those days, the sexes were often segregated, so it was not unusual for a hundred or so men to find themselves alone in remote, desolate lands, waiting for battles that never came, waiting for the day when they could once again delight in female companionship and discharge themselves of the urges building up during their isolation. Building. Building. Building. Ever building.

"So what did the men do about sex? They thought about it, they talked about it, and they dreamed about it. Some of them even did something about it.

"The exact nature of that something, as fate would have it, was uppermost in the mind of one General Dazelle, for it was a problem that he, too, would encounter while serving out his new assignment as commander of Base Hoyle. The general was a meticulous person who liked everything shipshape, and so upon his arrival to this remote military installation, he insisted the attaché take him on an immediate tour of the premises.

"The general was quite pleased with the barracks, the battlements, and the base as a whole, but he became quite distressed when he and the attaché turned a corner and saw hitched up to a post the sorriest, most pathetic, swaybacked, fly-infested old mare in the history of mankind. 'What—what is that—?' the general asked.

"'That is a mare,' said the attaché.

"'And why is it here? Why is it not stuffed and standing out in the field, scaring away the hawks and crows?'

"'Because the men need it, sir,' said the attaché.

"'Need it? What could they possibly need it for?'

"'Well, as you know, sir, the nearest civilian settlement is over a hundred kilometers away.'

"'Yes.'

"'And you know that, for security reasons, the only means of travel permitted for enlisted men between here and there is strictly bipedal.'

"'Yes, but I fail to see what any of that has to do with that failed genetic experiment.'

"'Well, then, surely you also know that men must be men. They have needs, you know. Needs that must be tended to.'

"The general looked in horror at the mare. He could not believe what he was hearing. The information was in grave danger of causing him severe psychological harm. 'You mean, the men—they—with that old mare?'

"The attaché nodded gravely. 'Yes. The urge builds up. There is nothing else they can do.'

"The general was on the verge of hyperventilating. He became so dizzy that he had to steady himself by leaning on the attaché. 'On my honor as a soldier,' said the general, 'I will never become that desperate.'

"But as his tour of duty wore on, the urge built and built, until one day he had no choice but to admit he was exactly that desperate. Finally he could take it no more, and he said to the attaché, 'Bring the mare to my quarters at once.'

"'To your quarters?' the attaché asked, evidently a little confused over something.

"'Yes, to my quarters,' said the general. 'You remember what you said, about the men—and the mare?'

"'Yes, sir!' said the attaché, saluting.

"The attaché did as he was told. By now the mare was, if anything, a mere shadow of her former decrepit self. Recently she had fallen off a cliff, and had been lucky to survive with only mildly crippling injuries, and her body had been ravaged by disease. So the attaché was quite horrified, stunned to the core of his being, in fact, when the general took off his trousers and began to have his way with the pathetic beast.

"'Sir!?' exclaimed the attaché, 'what are you doing?'

"'Is it not obvious what I am doing, sir?' said the general. 'Just as the men do!'

"'Sir, I fail to grasp your meaning,' said the attaché. 'Never, never have I seen such a sight.'

"'But, but, you said the men—their urges—and the mare . . .'

"'Sir, the men have their urges, it is true, but I meant that when the urges become too much for them, they climb on top of the mare and ride her to the nearest settlement.'

"There. Does that make everything clearer?" finished Harry.

"Wha' is he talkin' abou'?" mumbled Wolruf.

"Now I'm totally confused," whispered Derec. "At least his narrative technique is improving."

Ariel, meanwhile, couldn't stop laughing. "That—is the —silliest—thing I've ever heard," she said between breaths.

Harry remained in place on the stage as he awaited his audience's verdict. The robots had greeted the end of the joke with a kind of stony silence that only metal could summon. To a one, they stared straight ahead at Harry for several moments.

Then the robot that had asked the question that prompted the joke turned to its comrade on the right and said, "Yes, that makes sense."

"I understand," said another.

"As translucent as a gong," said a third.

"Mysterious, absolutely mysterious," said Canute.

The ebony was in the minority, however, as most of the robots seemed to be satisfied with Harry's explanation.

Derec waited for Ariel to stop laughing and asked her, "Just what do you think is going on here?"

She turned toward him, took him by the arm, and whispered in a conspiratorial tone, "The robots are beginning to learn about the world of Man the way we do—through jokes."

"That does not compute," replied Derec.

"Hmm. Let me put it this way. When you're growing up

on Aurora in the schools, one of the great mysteries in life is what's commonly known as the birds and bees."

"Yes, I know that phrase, but I don't recall how I learned about it."

"That's because you have amnesia. Now, listen, while we received a lot of classroom instruction in the scientific sense, we still had certain . . . anxieties. You don't remember yours, but you've probably still got a lot. Not that I'm being personal or anything, it's just a fact."

"Thank you. Go on."

"And one of the ways we kids relieved ourselves of our anxieties, and found out a little bit about reality, was through the artistic vehicle known throughout the galaxy as the dirty joke."

"And that's what's going on here?" Derec couldn't explain why, but he felt his face turning red. "This is an outrage! Should I put a stop to it?"

"Oh, you're such a prude. Of course not. This is all part of the learning experience. You know the old saying, 'Nobody approves of a dirty joke—except from someone who knows how to tell it.'"

"Then why am I going through all this effort to put on this big production? Why don't I just ask you to strip for them?"

"You'd like it, but they wouldn't care. They're not listening to these jokes for cheap thrills, but because they want to learn more about us."

"They really do. They really want to understand what it means to be human, don't they?"

"I think it's a lot different than that. Personally, though, I also think you should keep your mind on what's happening now, because Harry's launched into another joke."

Sure enough, the robot had. "The last man on Earth sat alone in a room," he was saying. "Suddenly, there was a knock on the door—"

"All right, you're a success, Harry." Waving his arms, Derec rushed up to him and put his hand over his speaker grill. A symbolic gesture, to be sure, but no less an effective one. "Just join your comrades backstage until I call for you, okay?"

"Yes, Mister Director," replied Harry, briskly walking away.

"Where were we? Oh, it doesn't matter. Let's talk about the play. 'The play's the thing,' Hamlet says, 'wherein I'll catch the conscience of the king.' Hamlet's uncle Claudius has murdered Hamlet's father, the King of Denmark, then taken his brother's place on the throne. To solidify his claim, Claudius has married Hamlet's mother, Gertrude. When Hamlet returns home from school, he has found the throne, which should be his, usurped, and while he suspects his uncle of foul play, he has no proof but the word of a ghost from beyond the grave.

"To secure this proof, Hamlet hires a traveling troupe of actors to perform a play that mirrors the crime that he believes Claudius has committed. He hopes that by watching his uncle during the performance, he'll see the guilt, the uncovered knowledge of the crime, written on his uncle's face.

"Claudius, meanwhile, suspects Hamlet of faking madness in search of this proof, and so he is stalking his nephew even as Hamlet is stalking him. The play is about the duel of wits between the two, and the means men will take to have what they want—be it a throne, revenge, or justice."

Derec turned to Mandelbrot and nodded. Mandelbrot stood and said, "The Mister Director wishes to thank you for volunteering and submitting to the interview process." Mandelbrot gestured toward Canute's way. "And for following orders. No doubt many orders will be curtly given you in the days to come, and Mister Director wishes to thank you in advance. As most of you know, Mister Director will assault the part of Hamlet, while Miss Ariel will impersonate the doomed, lamented Ophelia. I will now communicate on comlink wavelengths your assignments in the cast and crew categories."

It took Mandelbrot only a few seconds to do so, since he could impart more information so much more quickly on the higher frequencies. Derec and Ariel heard nothing; they only knew the robots were hearing because they often nodded to indicate their understanding.

"Okay, is everything understood?" Derec asked when Mandelbrot returned to his stiff sitting position.

Canute raised a finger. "Master, may I confer with you in private for a moment?"

"Sure," said Derec, walking stage right to the wings. "Come over here."

Canute did, and asked, "Master, am I to impart any significance to the fact that I have been assigned the role of Claudius?"

"No. Should there be?"

"It appears there should be. When you first spoke to me in the square, you asked questions of a nature I can only describe as suspicious. Soon afterward, you assigned me a task similar to the one Lucius took upon itself. And now, you assign me the role of a murderer—the object of the play-within-the-play. Surely the logical mind must be able to infer something from all this."

"Naw. Not at all, Canute. It's coincidence, sheer coincidence."

"May I inquire something further?"

"By all means."

"Why do you not just ask me forthrightly if I am the one responsible for Lucius's demise. You know I cannot withhold truth."

"Canute, I'm surprised at you. I've got no interest in asking you. Now get along. The best part's coming up next." Derec pushed the ebony in the direction of the robots, then rubbed his hands together as if to warm them with the help of a nearby fire. The ebony had dared a great deal in asking Derec to confront it. If Derec had taken up the dare, the game might have been over then and there, but the right answers to all his questions might never be found.

Mulling over the incident in the moment before he introduced the best part, Derec discovered that, despite himself, he was gaining a profound respect for Canute. Not approval, just respect. If found out, the ebony was a robot willing to face the consequences of its actions, but, in a way reminding Derec of human emotions, preferred to face them sooner than later.

"Many of you have probably heard of the human pastime of listening to music, and of those who make or record music, but I trust none of you have ever heard it before," said Derec to the cast and crew. "In fact, although I can't ever recall having personally heard music before, I daresay I've never heard it played in quite the way these three comrades play it.

"So I'd like to introduce to you the three comrades who will provide us with the incidental music of our production —Harry, Benny, and M334—The Three Cracked Cheeks of Robot City!"

Derec waved the three on as he walked behind Ariel. He whispered in her ear, "This ought to be good."

Benny stepped toward the proscenium of the stage as Harry and M334 put on their artificial lips. "Greetings, comrades. We thought we would perform an ancient Terran jingle called 'Tootin' Through the Roof.' Hope it stirs your coconut milk."

And The Three Cracked Cheeks began to play, at first an A-A-B-A riff theme with a solo by Benny on the trumpet. A solo from Harry on the trombone followed, and then M334 on the saxophone took over. In fact, it wasn't long before the solos were alternating thick and fast, with the two backers always offering support with the riff theme. The solos began to give the impression that the three were juggling a ball between them; and whoever had the ball had to depend on the other two for his foundation.

Derec hadn't heard the three play since that first audition. The first thing he noticed about this performance was their added confidence in themselves, the almost mathematical precision of the solo trade-offs, and the utter smoothness with which they assailed the tune. He looked down at his foot. It had been tapping.

He glanced at Ariel. He had expected her to be bored; her

contempt for all things Terran was, after all, the result of several generations' worth of cultural history. But instead of appearing bored, she looked directly at the three with rapt attention. Her foot was tapping, too.

"Now, thiss iss *Hamlet!*" said Wolruf.

CHAPTER 7
THE MEMORY OF DAWN

In two hours the performance would begin. Derec sat in his room, trying not to think about it. He was trying, in fact, not to think about much of anything. For though he had memorized practically the entire play, and felt as if he could perform his blocking blindfolded, he was afraid that if he ran through it in his mind now, at this late date, it would fall out of his memory as surely as his identity had.

After all, he had no idea what the cause of his amnesia was. It might have been caused by a severe blow to the head or a serious case of oxygen deprivation, but he could have some kind of disease as well—a disease that had caused him to lose his memory several times, forcing him to start over his search for his identity again and again. A disease that could strike again at any moment. Such as three minutes before the production was to begin.

Derec shrugged and lay down on his bed. Well, in such an eventuality, at least he would be spared the humiliation of embarrassment, he decided. He wouldn't remember anything or anybody.

The most terrible part of his fantasy—which he admitted was a little paranoid, but perhaps wasn't totally unwarranted under the circumstances—was that in the past he could have lost, time and time again, the companionship of intelligent beings who'd meant just as much to him as Ariel and Wolruf and Mandelbrot did now.

Maybe I should start thinking about the play, he thought. *It might be safer.*

The most important thing for him to remember was the secret purpose of the production, to watch Canute's reactions during the little surprises that Derec had cooked up for the robot.

For as Hamlet hoped to force Claudius to reveal his guilt while watching the play-within-the-play, Derec hoped Canute would at last be forced to confront its own true nature.

This was a nature Canute had steadfastly avoided confronting during rehearsals. When praised for its work in designing the theatre, Canute had admitted only that it was following orders, that it had given nothing of itself that was not logical. When it performed a scene particularly well during rehearsal, Canute had admitted only to following orders explicitly, to performing mechanically, as only a robot could.

But with luck, Canute had by now a case of robotic overconfidence. Derec's plans hinged on the hope that Canute believed it had already weathered the worse part of the investigation.

Of course, there was always the possibility that the surprises wouldn't work. What if they didn't? Then what would Derec have to do?

Derec realized he was wound up pretty tight. He relaxed with an effort. Then, when his thoughts began to turn automatically to the same matters, he tensed up again and had to relax with a second effort. Was this some form of stage fright? If it was, he supposed it could have been worse. He could be performing before humans.

There was a knock at the door. "Come in," he said, crossing his feet and putting his hands behind his head, so that whoever it was would think he was facing the coming performance with a mood of utter calm.

"Jumping galaxies! You look terrible!" said Ariel breathlessly as she closed the door behind her. "You must be nervous. It's good to know I'm not the only one."

Derec sat straight up and planted his feet on the floor. Just by being there, she had taken his breath away. She was in her costume—a blonde wig and a white gown that clung to her body as if it had been spun from a spider's web. Her makeup heightened the color of her cheeks and lips, and made her skin appear a healthier shade of pale. He hadn't realized that she could look so beautiful, with such an inner aliveness.

Of course, when he thought of all the circumstances that they had faced together—being thrown into a hospital together, running away from something, being stranded somewhere—it stood to reason that she had never before had the opportunity to accentuate her natural femininity. Her beauty in the costume was familiar, yet it was also something new, as if he'd glimpsed it in a long-forgotten dream.

But if she noticed his reaction (that is, if he revealed any of it), she gave no indication as she sat on the bed beside him. However, she glared at him because of his second reaction. It must have been none too flattering, for she looked like he had hit her over the head with a rubber chicken. "What's the matter with you?" she asked.

"What's that smell?" he replied.

"Oh, I had Mandelbrot synthesize some perfume for me. I thought it might help keep me in character."

"It's very pleasant."

"That's not what your face said at first."

"That's because I wasn't sure what I was smelling."

"Hmm. That's not much of a compliment. It's supposed to smell good whether or not you know what it is."

"Please, I've forgotten my social training along with the rest of my memory."

"Your face said it smelled like fertilizer."

"I'm not even sure I know what fertilizer smells like."

She pursed her lips and looked away from him, but he couldn't help noticing that her hand was very close to his on the bed. Their fingers were almost touching. "Nervous?" she asked.

He shrugged. "Naw. For all I know, this could be my first encounter with perfume."

"I meant the play, silly."

"Oh. Well, maybe a little. Hey, for all I know, I could be an old hand at this."

"I see. Do you think amnesia could sometimes be a blessing in disguise?"

"Ariel, something's bothering you. Are you well?"

"Reasonably well. Doing this play has given me something relatively constructive to concentrate on, though I'm still not sure it was a good idea for me to play someone who goes mad. I'm beginning to realize how uncomfortably it mirrors my own predicament."

"Would you rather play Hamlet's mother?"

"No. Well, maybe. But why couldn't I play Hamlet himself? I can be heard all over the stage, and you said so yourself, just yesterday, that I can definitely emote. Like crazy, if you'll forgive my choice of words."

"The role has been undertaken occasionally by women, according to the theatre history texts. I'm sure the robots would be only too positronically fulfilled to support you in a production of *Hamlet*. Or of any other play."

"I meant why couldn't I play Hamlet in *this* production?"

"Aha. You had your chance, but you volunteered to play Ophelia first! You were guilty of your own biased thinking —before I had the chance to engage in my biased thinking, that is."

"That's true," she replied, in tones a bit more serious than he thought his words warranted. "Besides, I think there're reasons why you picked *Hamlet,* beyond the ones that have to do with Canute. You could have picked any number of plays, you know, like *Othello* or *Julius Salad.*"

"That's *Julius Caesar!*"

"Right. Anyway, I think you already saw a lot of yourself in him—the mad romantic, the soul-searching adventurer, the vain, pompous, arrogant, stubborn . . . stubborn . . ."

"Egotist."

"Right. Egotist."

Derec smiled. It was exciting to have her sitting next to him. Except for rehearsing bits of business together, they hadn't been this close for some time, and he was surprised to discover how much he liked it. He was nervous and relaxed at the same time.

"Derec? Pay attention. I'm talking to you," she said gently. "Listen, I've been thinking about the differences between us and the people back then, or the way they were presented, anyway. I can't help but wonder if anyone today ever has the kind of love Ophelia has for Hamlet."

"Or Lady Macbeth has for Macbeth?"

"I'm serious. I know Ophelia is definitely a weak creature. 'Hi there, Dad. Use me as a pawn in your nefarious schemes. Please?' But for all that, she really does love with a consuming passion. I've never met any one on Aurora who's felt that kind of love . . . that I know of, naturally. But I think I would be able to tell if there were any Ophelias out there."

"How about yourself?" he asked with an unexpected catch in his voice.

"Me? No, I've never felt that kind of passion." She narrowed her eyes as she looked at him. He couldn't help but wonder what she was really thinking as she pulled away from him, put her foot on the bed, and rested her head on her knee. "I've had sex, of course, and crushes, but nothing like what Ophelia must feel." She paused, buried her face in her gown, then lifted her head just enough so he could see her raise an eyebrow. With a decidedly interesting intent. "I might be persuaded to try, though."

Derec felt a lump the size of a sidewalk get stuck in his throat. "Ariel!"

"Derec—are you a virgin?"

"How am I supposed to know? I have amnesia!" Now it was his turn to raise his eyebrows, as she moved closer to him.

"You know, there's another aspect to Ophelia," she said. "She represents something." Closer. "Something Hamlet needs but which he has to deny to have his revenge."

"He was a user, too."

"How about that." Closer.

She leaned forward. He kissed her. No, he couldn't remember having felt anything quite like this before. Feeling obligated to pursue the matter scientifically, though, he felt confident he might remember after a little more experimentation.

"Wait," she said after a time, pushing away. "I'm sorry. I got carried away there. I'm not always in control of myself."

"Uh, that's all right," he replied, suddenly feeling slightly embarrassed.

"That's not the point. It's my medical condition. Don't be offended, but right now I'm feeling a little *healthier* than common sense tells me I should. Remember how I acquired my little condition."

"Don't worry. I won't forget," he said, drawing her toward him to kiss her again. Their lips were millimeters apart when there was an insistent knocking at the door. "Damn!" he whispered in response. "It must be the Brain Police!"

"Master Derec?" said a stone cold, metallic voice outside. "Mistress Ariel?" It was the voice of a hunter robot.

"Yes? What is it?" Derec shouted. Then in a whisper. "See? I was right, in a way."

"Mandelbrot sent me to locate you and remind you that you should depart for the New Globe soon. There are a few details that only you can provide."

"All right," Derec said. "We'll be there soon."

"Very good, sir," said the Hunter robot, its voice already fading.

"What did you say?" she asked. "Brain Police."

"I don't know. It just popped into my head."

"If I remember correctly, the Brain Police are something from some children's holodrama I saw when I was growing up. It's famous. They're from—from that series called *Tyrants of Blood.*"

Derec was amazed. "About a masked man who rescues helpless thought deviants on a totalitarian planet. I remember. Is that a clue to my identity?"

"I doubt it. I said it was famous—and it was syndicated, seen all over the known systems. It's been playing for generations."

"Oh. So it means nothing."

"No, it means at least we can be sure you're from some civilized world."

"Thanks a lot. Come on. Our public awaits."

CHAPTER 8
TO BE, OR WHAT?

"Master, if my understanding of human nature is correct, you'll be happy to know that we have a full house," said Mandelbrot.

"Thanks, but I saw them lining up on my way in," said Derec as he hastily donned the tight breeches that were a part of his costume. He waited until he had put on the remainder of his costume—a purple tunic over a white shirt with ruffled sleeves, and a pair of boots—before he asked Mandelbrot, "How's Canute? Has it done anything unusual —anything that might indicate it knows about my special plans?"

"So far it appears to be acting like the rest of the robots. That is, as calm as ever."

"You're not nervous at all, are you?"

"I am naturally concerned that the illusion proceeds as planned, as are all the robots, but the only nervousness I might possess, if I may use such a word as 'nervousness,' revolves around my concern that you perform in accordance with your own standards."

"Thanks. How much time do we have?"

"Mere moments until curtain."

"Everything in place?"

"Everything but your greasepaint, master."

"My makeup! I forgot all about it."

Mandelbrot helped him apply it, in great heaps that Derec was certain would appear primitive and grotesquely over-stated when picked up by the cameras. "Is the stage ready?" Derec asked. "Everything in its proper place?"

"Naturally."

"But the Hunter said—"

"Forgive me, master, but I deduced how you would want the remaining details handled."

Derec nodded, but said nothing. Suddenly he was gripped by the overriding fear that he would step out on stage and forget every single one of his lines. Or worse, he would begin acting out the wrong scene.

"Relax, master. I am confident you will perform to the letter."

Derec smiled. He looked in the mirror. He hoped he looked fine. Then he walked out into the wings, joining Ariel and the robots.

Wolruf sat on a special chair in the very rear section of the backstage area, before a bank of screens showing the stage from several angles. Three supervisor robots sat in chairs before the screens, operating automatic cameras concealed throughout the theatre that, with appropriate zooms and pans would provide a total picture of everything on stage. All that was left was for Wolruf to call the shots and to tell one of the robots what should be broadcast to the holoscreens throughout the city.

Beside her was a huge dish of artificial roughage. Though her concentration was on the screens, she was absent-mindedly, systematically picking up handfuls and stuffing them into her mouth.

If she had a tail, Derec thought, *she'd be wagging it in happiness.*

"Master, it's curtain time!" said Mandelbrot.

Derec raised an eyebrow. "Mandelbrot! Is that a quiver of excitement I detect in your voice?"

Mandelbrot shook his head—Derec couldn't tell if it was from confusion or from a desire to communicate an emphatic *no*. "That would be impossible." He straightened and paused. "Unless I've assimilated some of your lessons on voice inflection, and have begun using them without conscious knowledge."

"Later, Mandelbrot, later. Let's get this show on the, uh,

road." He gave a signal to a stagehand, and the curtain rose.

A single shaft of light revealed the robot playing Francisco, the guard at his post, standing in the center of the stage. The robot playing Bernardo entered and said, "Who's there?"

Francisco stood straight, gestured with his spear, and said in authoritative tones, "Nay, answer me; stand, and unfold yourself."

At the moment, Derec could not recall a single one of his lines, not even those of the difficult soliloquy, but now he felt confident that he would know what to do and what to say when the time came. He steeled himself, realizing that he would have to forget about being Derec What's-his-name for a while. For the next three hours, he would be somebody else, somebody called Hamlet, Prince of Denmark.

Indeed, once he stepped into the stream, Derec was rushed headlong down the events of the play as if he had been swept up by rapids. He even forgot to spring some of his surprises on Canute, slight line changes reflecting the events of the past few weeks that, presumably, were subtle enough that only Canute would grasp their import and realize Derec was planning to put him on the spot. Derec eventually signaled Mandelbrot that he was calling off that entire aspect of his plot, because to change the play at this point, even for a good reason, seemed almost criminal.

All the robots performed brilliantly, with perfect precision. Derec realized that his fears the show might be unsuccessful were ungrounded, at least on that score. For he was dealing with robots, not humans who might vary their performances from time to time. Once the robots had grasped Derec's meanings during rehearsal, they had never deviated from them. And tonight was no exception.

Needless to say, Canute had given away nothing during rehearsal. But tonight, during the performance, he played his role beautifully, almost brilliantly. He played Claudius as Derec would have liked to have instructed him to play the role, but had refrained for fear of tipping too much of his hand. Tonight Canute was arrogant, controlled, self-assured, guilt-ridden, and obsessed with holding onto what he imagined was rightfully his.

It was almost as if, having decided that it would weather the production without being exposed, Canute had mentally relaxed and had permitted itself to be swept down the same rapids.

Good, Derec thought during the second scene of the third act. *Then the big surprise should work even more effectively.*

For this was the scene of the play-within-the play, and before the "actors" began their "real" performance, the script called for a dumbshow, a play without words, that mirrored the action of *Hamlet.* In the original, a king and queen passionately embrace, and then the queen leaves as the king sleeps. A third party enters, takes off the king's crown and then pours poison into his ears. When the queen returns, she grieves for her dead husband, then is wooed by the poisoner, who quickly wins her love.

Derec figured that a rewrite of a pantomine was all right, since it didn't involve changing any dialogue. Besides, he'd read in the foreword to the text that Shakespeare's plays had been frequently tampered with to make them more relevant (or seemingly so) to the world of the production.

But in the rewrite, the king built a tall building of sticks and cogs, to the tune of "Blue Goose." The queen admired it, then left. And as the king gazed down upon his creation, the third party snuck up behind him and bashed him over the head with a big stick. The king fell down dead, and then the third party smashed the building. The Three Cracked Cheeks played "Stormy Weather."

Derec applauded to indicate the dumbshow was over. When Ariel looked at him, asking with her eyes what was happening, Derec merely shrugged, but watched Canute as he said his lines. After the actors resumed their performance, Canute acted out the scenes of Claudius's guilt no differently than before, after making allowances for the robot's more "relaxed" attitude.

The rest of the play continued without special event. It

proceeded until Hamlet died, Derec landing on the floor with a resounding thud, feeling pretty dead inside himself. Poor Lucius! The first creative robot in history was going to be unavenged.

Well, I'm not through yet, thought Derec, lying on the floor as the robots wrapped up the last scene of the play. *I can literally take Canute apart if I want to—and I think I will.*

Derec stood up as the curtain fell and looked at everyone in anticipation. "Well—how do you think it went?"

"Forgive me, master," said Canute, drawing itself up to its full height almost like a prideful human, "but if you will permit a subjective opinion, I think the production was an utter failure."

CHAPTER 9
THE COMPANY HAS COMPANY

"What do you mean, this play has been a failure?" demanded a livid Ariel. "The production was smooth, very believable," she added, looking at Derec.

At the moment Derec was too busy being defensive to respond verbally, but he nodded gratefully. Most of the cast and crew had gathered around them behind the curtain, and nearly all were talking to one another. Things were too jumbled for Derec to make much sense of it. He was feeling lost, anyway. The play was over, and he had to go back to being his real self.

"Quiet, everyone, listen!" said Canute in raised tones.

They obeyed, and heard only silence from the audience hidden by the curtain.

"You see?" said Canute after a moment. "There is no response whatsoever. I have been vindicated: robots are not artistic, nor can they respond to art. It is perhaps unfortunate that your friend Lucius cannot be here to notice."

"Forgive me, friend Canute," said Harry, "but you have overlooked one fact: no one has ever mentioned to robots how they should respond. If I know my fellows, they are sitting there in their chairs, wondering what they should do next."

Benny said, "Excuse me, I must communicate through my comlink."

A few seconds later the house was filled with thunderous metallic applause. It went on and on and on.

M334 gestured to a stagehand to raise the curtain so the

cast could take a bow. And as the cast did so, Harry said to Canute, "You see? They liked it!"

"They are merely being polite," said Canute without conviction.

"Congratulations, master," said Mandelbrot. "It seems the play is a success."

Derec couldn't resist a smile, though whether it was because of the play or because an overjoyed Ariel was hugging him, he couldn't say. "I just hope it came off as well on the holoscreens."

"It should have," said Ariel. "I told Wolruf to concentrate on my best profile. The robots should be mesmerized by my beauty forever!"

They won't be the only ones, Derec thought as he and the cast and crew took the first of several bows.

Still the applause went on and on; it seemed it would never stop.

But suddenly it did, and the robots all turned their heads around as a diminutive figure walked down an aisle.

A diminutive *human* figure, a stunned Derec realized.

A figure who was a roundish man with baggy trousers, an oversized coat, and a white shirt with a ruffled collar. He had long wavy white hair and a bushy mustache, and an intense expression that implied he was capable of remarkable feats of concentration. When he reached the bottom of the aisle, he stopped, stared angrily at the people and robots on stage, put his arms to his hips, and said, "What is going on here? What kind of game are you playing with my robots?"

"By the seven galaxies!" Derec exclaimed. "You must be Dr. Avery!"

"Who else?" the man asked.

CHAPTER 10
ALL ABOUT AVERY

"I want to see you—you—you—and you," said Avery, walking onstage and pointing in turn at Derec, Ariel, Wolruf, and Mandelbrot. "Is there some place in this rather grandiose structure where we can meet in private?"

Almost immediately, Derec decided there was something he didn't like about the man. No, he had to take that back. Something about Avery made Derec feel uncomfortable and uncharacteristically meek. Perhaps it was Avery's air of cool superiority, or the manner in which he assumed his authority would be taken for granted.

Even so, Derec decided that cooperation was his best option for the moment. Avery must have gotten here somehow; his Key to Perihelion could take Ariel away, or perhaps his ship would be large enough for more than one person, so at least Ariel would have the chance to get the medical help Derec had so far been unable to provide. For that reason, if for no other, Derec steeled himself and said, "We can go to my dressing room, backstage."

Avery nodded, as if deeply considering the serious ramifications of the suggestion. "Excellent."

In the room, Avery calmly demanded to know who everyone was, and how they had gotten there. Derec saw no reason to conceal the truth, at least the greater portion of it. He told Avery how he had awoken bereft of memory in the survival pod on the mining colony, how he had discovered Ariel, and how they had made their way to Robot City. He described his encounter with the alien who had instructed him to build Mandelbrot, and how Wolruf had broken away from her servitude. He told Avery how he had deduced the flaw in the programming that was causing the city to self-destruct by expanding at an insupportable speed, how they had found a murdered body that was an exact duplicate of Derec, and how he and Ariel had saved the marooned Jeff from becoming a paranoid schizophrenic for the rest of his life when his brain had been placed in a robot's body. Finally, he recounted what little he had learned about Lucius; and how Lucius had created Circuit Breaker the same night of the robot's untimely demise.

"That's when I decided to put on a performance of *Hamlet*," said Derec, "in order to uncover the killer. But so far it seems my schemes have had no effect on the robot Canute, so I still have no idea why it did what I suspect it did. I've no proof, however, that even my theory is correct. I guess when all is said and done, I just hadn't thought things through enough."

Avery nodded, but said nothing. His expression was rather stern, but otherwise noncommittal. Derec really had no idea of how Avery was reacting to the chronicling of all these events.

"So you programmed this city all by yourself?" said Ariel casually. She was sitting on a couch with her legs crossed, still in costume. The effect was rather disconcerting, since although she had dropped her character completely, Derec was still visually cued to think of her as Ophelia. "I bet you never suspected for a moment that it would take on all these unprecedented permutations."

"What I suspected would happen is my business," replied Avery as tonelessly as a robot.

"Iss tha' rud-ness nexessaree?" said Wolruf. "Esspecially to one who did so much to presserrve 'ur inven'shon."

"Preserve it?" said Avery incredulously. Suddenly he began pacing back and forth around the room in an agitated fashion. "It remains to be seen whether my designs have been preserved or not. One thing is clear, though, and that's that something unusual is going on, something I think you may have made even worse."

"Forgive me if I seem presumptuous," said Mandelbrot, who was standing next to the doorway, "but logic informs me that it is your absence that has had the most undesirable effect on the city. My master and his friends did not wish to come here or to stay, and they have dealt with the developments as best they knew how. Indeed, logic also informs me that perhaps your absence was part of your basic plan."

Avery glared at the robot. "Close down," he said curtly.

"No, Mandelbrot, you shall do nothing of the sort. That is a direct order." Derec looked at Avery. "He is mine, and his first allegiance is to me."

Avery smiled. "But all the other robots in the city owe their first allegiance to me. I could have them enter and dismantle him if I wished."

"That is very true," said Ariel. "But what would you say if I told you that one of your robots has a desire to be a stand-up comedian?"

Wolruf said, "Wheneverr hear joke, know firrss' hand trrue meanin' of sufferrin'."

"I have no qualms about attesting to that," said Mandelbrot.

"You're irrational—all of you!" Avery whispered.

"I've been meaning to talk to you about that," said Ariel.

"I see," said Avery. "I know you—the Auroran who had the liaison with a Spacer."

"And I was contaminated as a result," said Ariel. "Does this mean I've become famous? I'm not ashamed of what I did—but then again, I'm not especially proud of my disease, either. I'm slowly going mad, and I've got to get off this world to obtain the proper medical attention."

"I could use some myself," said Derec. "I'd like to know who I am."

"Naturally," said Avery. But he said nothing else, and the others waited for several seconds, each thinking that he would add the words they hoped to hear. "But I have other plans," he finally said off-handedly.

"What other plans?" Derec exclaimed, making a frantic gesture. "What could possibly be more important than getting Ariel to a doctor?"

But Avery said nothing. He merely sat down in a chair and crossed his legs. He rubbed his face and then ran his hand through his hair. His brows knitted as if he was concentrating deeply, but exactly about what remained a mystery.

"Excuse me, Dr. Avery, but being examined by a diagnostic robot was no help," said Ariel. "I need human attention as quickly as possible."

"Perhaps a diagnostic robot native to the city will better know what to look for," said Avery, "which after all is half the battle when it comes to medicine."

"Unfortunately, Dr. Avery, that seems not to be the case," said Mandelbrot. "Mistress Ariel was examined by Surgeon Experimental 1 and Human Medical Research 1 during the recuperation of Jeff Leong from his experimental surgery. They were able to determine only that her illness was beyond their abilities of diagnosis and treatment. They have not been affected by the strangely intuitive thinking that is rapidly becoming endemic in this place, possibly because they were first activated after the near-disaster from which Master Derec saved Robot City."

"You're sure of that?" Derec asked.

"Not as to the cause, but that they have remained as they were, yes. I have maintained regular contact with them," the robot responded. "They are working on the blood and tissue samples that Mistress Ariel left with them, but have made no breakthroughs."

"Then I was right." Derec pounded a fist into his other hand. "The only way we can make any progress on a cure is if we add one of the intuitive robots to the medical team."

"I don't think so," said Avery coldly. "In fact, all this so-called intuitive thinking is going to come to a halt rather quickly, as soon as I figure out how to stop it. It's too unpredictable. It must be studied under controlled conditions. Strictly controlled conditions, without robots running around telling jokes."

"That's just too bad," said Derec. "Ariel is going to be cured, one way or the other, and there's nothing you can do to stop me."

Avery's eyes widened. Staring silently at Derec for several moments, he rapped his fingers on the makeup table and crossed and uncrossed his feet. The actions weren't nervous, but they were agitated. "Friend Derec, this city is mine. I created it. I own it. There is no one who understands it better than me."

"Then you should be able to explain quite easily some of the things that have been going on here," Derec snapped.

Avery dismissed the notion with a wave. "Oh, I will, when it's convenient."

"Iss that why 'u crreated it?" Wolruf asked pointedly, her lip curling.

"And I can dissect you if I wish," replied Avery evenly. "The fact that you're the first alien in human captivity almost demands it as the proper scientific response."

"Don't even think about it!" said Derec. "First, Wolruf isn't in captivity; she's our friend. We won't let you so much as X-ray her without her express permission. Understand?"

"The robots accept me as their primary master, and I bet they've already decided that she isn't human. After all, she doesn't remotely look or act human."

"But she is as intelligent as a human, and a robot would certainly be influenced by that," countered Derec. "Your robots just might find themselves unable to complete your orders."

"Only the more intelligent ones," said Avery. "There are many grades of intelligence here, and I can restrict my orders to the lowest forms in the eventuality of any conflicts in that area."

"I think you're underestimating his ability to take control," countered Ariel for Derec.

Avery smiled. "Your friend seems to have great confidence in you," he said to Derec. "I hope it is justified."

"I wouldn't have gotten as far as I have without some ability to turn an unfortunate development around to my advantage," said Derec.

"He'ss had help," said Wolruf.

"I, too, have assisted him, as much as robotically possible," said Mandelbrot, "and shall continue to do so as long as I am functioning. Thanks to Master Derec, I have learned much of what human beings mean by the word 'friend'."

Avery nodded. He scrutinized Derec with what appeared to be a peculiar combination of pride and anger. It was as if Avery could not make up his own mind about how he felt about this crew and what he wanted to do about them. Derec had the distinct feeling that this man was flying without a navigation computer.

"How did you get here?" asked Derec.

"That is my business and none of yours."

"Did you perchance find a Key to Perihelion? In that case, it wouldn't inconvenience you in the least to permit Ariel and me to use it. I would return as soon as she was being taken care of."

"I don't know that, and in any case your suggestion is immaterial. I have no such Key."

"Then you've arrived in a spacecraft," said Derec, forcing the issue in an effort to do exactly what he had been doing since he had awakened in the survival pod: turn things around to his advantage. "Where is it?"

Avery laughed uproariously. "I'm not going to tell you!"

"It is ironic, is it not," said Mandelbrot, "that humans, who depend so much upon robots to adhere to the Three Laws, cannot be programmed to obey them."

"Thiss one exis'ss ou'side lawss of 'ur kind," said Wolruf.

Avery regarded the alien in a new light. "If what you're saying means what I think it does, then you're absolutely correct."

"Is this how you get your kicks," asked Derec, "by jeopardizing the lives of innocent people?"

Now a light of an entirely different sort blazed in Avery's eyes. "No, by *disregarding* the lives of innocent people. The only thing that matters is my work. And my work would never get done if I allowed my behavior to be restricted by so-called humanitarian considerations."

"Is that why you left the city for so long, to get your work done? To start other colonies?" Derec asked.

"I was away, and that is all you need to know." Avery put his hand in his pocket, pulled out a small device and pointed it at Mandelbrot. The device resembled a pinwheel, but it made a strange hissing sound when it moved, and the sparks, instead of coming out of the wheel, came out of Mandelbrot!

Ariel screamed.

"What are you doing to him?" Derec asked, rushing to his robot's side.

Wolruf squatted, and her hindquarters twitched as if she was about to make a leap at Avery. Avery looked at her and said, "Careful. I can make it easier on him—or I can make it worse!"

Wolruf straightened up, but she warily kept her eye on Avery, searching for an opportunity to strike.

Derec was so angry that his intentions were the same, though he was hoping he wasn't being that obvious about it. But at the moment he was preoccupied with trying to keep Mandelbrot standing, or at least leaning against the wall, though he wasn't sure what difference it would make.

Mandelbrot quivered as the sparks spat out of his joints and every opening in his face. His pseudo-muscular coordination was in an advanced state of disruption; his arms and legs flailed spastically and an eerie moan rose from his speaker grill like a ghostly wail. Derec pushed him flat against the wall, and was struck several times by the robot's uncontrollable hands and elbows. Despite Derec's efforts, however, Mandelbrot slid onto the floor, and Derec sat on him, trying to keep the writhing robot down. But Mandelbrot was too strong, and finally it was all Derec could do to get out of harm's way.

Avery, meanwhile, calmly continued to point the device at the robot. "Don't come any closer—I can make it worse. I can even induce positronic drift."

"What are you doing to him?" Derec repeated.

"This is an electronic disrupter, a device of my own invention," Avery replied with some pride. "It emits an ion stream that interferes with the circuits of any sufficiently advanced machine."

"You're hurting him!" said Ariel. "Don't you care?"

"Of course not, my dear. This is a robot, and hence has only the rights I prefer to bestow upon him."

"Think not!" growled Wolruf.

"I can press a button faster than any of you can move," said Avery, warningly.

"Why are you doing this?" Derec asked.

"Because I do not wish this robot to interfere. You see, I have stationed some Hunter robots outside this theatre. They await my signal, even as we speak. When I alert them, they will capture you and take you to my laboratory, where I shall drug you with an advanced truth serum and learn everything your mind has to tell me."

"Will this serum help me remember who I am?"

"Derec!" exclaimed Ariel, shocked.

"I seriously doubt it. Unfortunately, the serum isn't quite perfected yet—it's another invention of mine—and I confess there is the possibility that it may actually jumble things up a little more for you. For a time, anyway. You may take comfort in the fact that the damage won't be permanent."

Derec nodded. He looked at Mandelbrot on the floor. "Sorry, old buddy," he said.

"What?" said Avery, a nanosecond before Derec hefted a chair at him.

As the scientist ducked, Derec ran to the door, shouting, "Follow me! We'll come back for Mandelbrot later!"

The trio ran down the hall toward the stage, toward members of the cast and crew. Wolruf was clearly holding herself back to remain with Derec and Ariel.

"Out of the way!" Derec shouted as they moved past the

robots; he hoped that he could create enough confusion to slow down the robots in case Avery invoked his precedential authority and ordered them to capture him and his friends.

"Where are we going?" Ariel asked.

"You'll see!"

They soon heard Avery angrily shouting something in the background, but by then they had reached the stage. Derec stopped at the center trapdoor and opened it. "Quick! Down here!"

"But that leads backstage!" protested Ariel.

"That's not all," said Derec. "Hurry!"

Wolruf leapt inside, and Derec and Ariel were quickly with her. As Derec closed the door, they were enveloped in blackness. "We'll have to feel our way around for a few minutes," said Derec as they made their way down the narrow corridor. "Ah! Here! This door leads to the underground conduits of the city! Even Avery's Hunters will have a hard time searching for us down here!"

"Not for long!" said Ariel. "Can't they trace us with infrared?"

"It'll still give us time!" said Derec between his teeth. "And we can use that time to figure out our next move! Let's go!"

"All right," said Ariel resignedly, "but I hope somebody turns on the lights."

As it happened, the lights were the one thing they didn't have to worry about. The lining of the underground conduits automatically glowed in the presence of visitors, illuminating the narrow spaces several meters behind and ahead of them. Things were not so elegant here. At first they saw only what they had expected: wires and cables, pipes, circuit banks, transistorized power generators, oscillators, stress and strain gauges, capacitors, fusion pods, and various other devices that Derec, for all his knowledge in electronics and positronics, could not even name. He stared at the construction in fascination, momentarily forgetting the reason why he and his friends had come here.

Derec couldn't help but admire Avery. Surely the man

was a genius unparalleled in human history; it was too bad he appeared to have lost his humanity in the process of making his dreams real.

"How much further do we have to go?" Ariel finally asked. "I'm getting tired, and it's not too easy to get around in this silly dress."

"I don't know," said Derec, breathing heavily. He hadn't realized how tired he was. He had given all his energy to the performance, and probably didn't have too much reserve left at the moment. "We could keep going, I suppose, but I don't see what difference it'd make."

"More be'ween 'u an' 'ur purrsuerrs, the bedder," said Wolruf. "Firss less-on pup learrns."

"Derec—what's that?" Ariel asked, pointing to the illuminated regions ahead.

"What's what? Everything looks the same."

Wolruf sniffed the air. "Smell not the same."

Derec moved up the corridor. As he did so, the illumination moved upward with him. And in the distance, just before the corridor was enveloped in total darkness, wires and generators began to blend into an amorphous form. Derec waved the others on. "Let's go—I want to see what's going on."

"Derec, we're in trouble—we can't go exploring just because we feel like it."

"I don't know why not. Besides, this corridor only goes in two directions—this way and that way."

The further they went, the more amorphous the materials in the conduit became, merging into one another until only the vaguest outlines of generators, cables, fusion pods, and all the other parts were visible. It was as if every aspect of the conduit had been welded into inseparable parts. Derec had the feeling that if he could open one of the generators, for example, what he would find inside would be amorphous, fused circuits and wires.

"Deeper," he said, "we've got to go deeper."

"Derec, things are definitely getting cramped here," protested Ariel.

"She's rite," said Wolruf. "Furr'her down we go, the narrower the tunnel. If Hunterrs come—"

"We won't be able to do anything anyway," said Derec. "Look at what's happening here! Don't you realize what's going on?"

"Looks like the city's beginning to dissolve," said Ariel.

"Ah! In actuality, the effect is precisely the opposite. The further up we go, the more the city begins to coalesce. Understand?"

"Are you serious? No!"

"The ultimate foundation of Robot City is still further down this conduit. The meta-cells must be manufactured below, and they're propelled upward in much the same way that water's propelled through a pipe. Only more slowly."

"Then why are all these phony machines here?"

"They're not phony, they just haven't been fully formed yet. The cells probably have to make it through a certain portion of the foundation before they can really begin to get with their program. You see, the atoms of metal form a lattice in three dimensions, which is why metals occur in polycrystalline form—that is, large numbers of small crystals. The cells in this part of the underground haven't crystallized yet. Ariel?"

She had looked away. She was nodding as if she understood his explanation, but her face was perspiring, and she had grown noticeably paler, even in the dim light. Derec reached for her as if to steady her, but she pulled away from him.

"Don't—" she said, waving him away. "I—I'm getting claustrophobic. It's too narrow in here. I—I'm feeling all this weight on top of me."

"Don't worry about it," said Derec. "The foundation is secure. Nothing's going to happen."

"What are we going to do if the Hunters come?"

"They may not be able to find us here. Even with infrared sensors. If the program's not complete in this sector, then it's possible that they won't be able to detect us."

"Only possibly," said Wolruf. "Even if they don' come,

we'll hav' to leave sooner orr la'err. Then they find us."

Now Derec waved them both away. "All right, all right. I know all this. I'm sorry."

"U could no' help ur-self."

Derec snorted, which was about as close to a self-mocking laugh as he could muster at the moment. It was bad enough that they had come to a literal dead end—they had arrived at the end of the road in more ways than one.

How he wished Mandelbrot was with them now! He felt like a callous coward, having left him behind that way. He had left in the hope that he would be able to come back for the robot, but now he feared Avery would dismantle the brain and scatter the parts all over the city, thus making it possible to rebuild him only if all the parts could be found.

Derec looked at his open palms. He had put Mandelbrot together with these hands and his brain, from the spare parts he'd had available. Now his hands and brain seemed hopelessly inadequate to cope with the problems besetting him. He could not help Ariel. He could not help Wolruf and Mandelbrot. He had been unable to make Canute confess and to bring the robot to whatever kind of justice might be appropriate. Hell, he may not even have solved the question of who killed Lucius in the first place. Last—but at the moment the very least—he had been unable to help himself.

Wolruf made a gurgling sound deep in her throat. "Derec, a prroblem."

"Another one?"

"Oh, yes!"

Derec looked up to see, at the edge of the darkness above them, the Hunter robots advancing.

CHAPTER 11
DREAMS OUT OF JOINT

Derec awoke in a place that he knew was not real. Otherwise, he had no idea where he was. He stood on a smooth copper plane extending unbroken in all directions. Above him was a pitch-black sky. Theoretically, he should have been engulfed in darkness as well, since the copper was hardly an obvious source of illumination, but vision was no problem.

In fact, Derec realized, his range of sight extended into the ultraviolet and infrared range. When he looked down to inspect his hand, his neck joints creaked: he would not have been able to hear that sound if he had been human. For he was now a robot. His metal hand proved that beyond doubt.

Normally, such a turn of events would have sent him into a fit of deep depression, but, now that the deed was done, Derec accepted it quite readily. He did not know why or how he had changed, nor did he think the reasons mattered much. All that remained was for him to figure out what he wanted to do next.

Logically, he should walk. Since there was no logical way to determine if one direction was preferable to any other, he simply started off in the direction he happened to be facing.

And as he walked, he saw that something was growing in the distance. He walked more quickly, hoping to reach his destination that much faster, but it always remained the same distance away.

So he ran, and the something seemed to glide across the

copper surface away from him, maintaining the distance between them.

He saw that at the upper regions of the something were the spires of a city, streaking against the sky as the foundation glided away. Streaking against the sky and cutting through it, tearing it, exposing the whiteness beyond. Ribbons of whiteness dangled from the nothingness, and though Derec could not reach the city, eventually he did stand directly beneath the ribbons. Reason told him that they were far away, probably at least a kilometer above him, but he gave in to the urge to reach out and touch one.

He grabbed it, and felt a flash of searing heat blaze through his soul. He tried to scream, but could not make a sound.

He tried to release the ribbon, but it clung to his fingers. It expanded. It enveloped him, smothering the copper and the blackness of the world.

Or was he falling inside the ribbon? It was hard to tell. Reason also began to tell him that this was a dream of some sort that he was living, and that it would be better if he went along with it and tried not to fight it. Perhaps his mind was trying to tell him something.

He fell through the whiteness until he came to a school of giant amoebae, but instead of being creatures of proteins they were composed of circuits laid out like a lattice. He kicked his legs and waved his arms, and discovered that he could swim the currents of whiteness just as they could. He swam with them . . .

. . . Until they swept 'round and 'round in circles, disappearing into a point in the whiteness as if it was the center of a whirlpool. Derec tried to swim against the current, but he was inexorably pulled down into the point.

He came out on the other side, surrounded not by amoebae, but by molten ore rapidly being solidified into meteors by the near-absolute-zero temperatures in this space. Now he was in a void where there was no current to swim. He thought that he should be afraid, yet he was facing the situation with incredible calm. Perhaps that was because in this dream he was a robot both in mind and in body His body was unaffected by the cold, and he required no air to breathe, so, except for the danger of being struck by a solidifying slag heap, he was in no danger. Hence he had nothing to fear, nothing to worry about.

Nothing, perhaps, except for where he might be going. He wished he could resist the trajectory he was taking, but there was nothing he could do about it, for there was nothing for him to grab onto or to kick against. He had no choice but to submit to his momentum, and hope to be able to act later.

He had no way to judge how much time had passed when he plummeted from the void into a dark-blue sky, nor could he explain how he had managed to fall so far, so fast, without bursting into flames upon his entry into the atmosphere.

He landed in a vast sea, and swam to a shore where the waves pounded against the rocks. He crawled onto the beach, feeling as strong and as fit as when he had first began this dream, but now a bit afraid that he might rust. However, once he had walked away from the beach and could once again see the city in the distance, his metal body was perfectly dry, and none the worse for wear.

He walked toward the city. Now it remained stationary, and the closer he came to it, the more brilliant it gleamed in the sunlight, with rainbow colors that glistened as if the towers and pyramids and flying buttresses were sparkling with the fresh dew of morning.

And inside the boundaries of the city were buildings shaped like hexagonal prisms, ditetragonal prisms, dodecahedrons, and hexoctahedrons—complex geometric shapes all, but each with its own purity arising from its simplicity. Yet there seemed to be nothing inside the buildings; there were no doors, no windows, no entrances of any kind. The colors of the buildings glistened in the sunlight: crimson, wheat, ochre, sapphire, gold, sable, and emerald, each and every one so pleasing to his logic integrals, all so constant and pure.

Yet the deeper he walked into the city, the fewer buildings there were. They were spaced further apart, until the emptiness formed a tremendous square in the center. And in the square was an array of mysterious machinery, surrounded by transparent plastic packages of dry chemicals scattered on the ground. They all seemed to be asking to be used.

But for what?

Derec did use them. He did not know why, nor did he know exactly how he used them. He mixed the contents of the plastic packages into the machinery when it seemed appropriate; in fact, he rebuilt the machines when it was appropriate. Again, he did not know exactly why or how he accomplished this. It was only a dream, after all.

And when he was done he stood at the edge of the square and looked upon the opening he had made in the fabric of the universe. Inside he saw clusters of galaxies swirling, moving apart in a stately, steady flow. Gradually, they moved beyond his point of view, but instead of leaving utter blackness in their wake, they left a blinding white light.

Derec happily stepped inside the light. It was time to awaken, for now he knew how to reach Canute.

CHAPTER 12
THE THEORY OF EVERYTHING

"Wake up, my lad," came the voice of Dr. Avery from behind the veil of blackness. "The time has come to join the land of the living."

Derec opened his eyes. Dr. Avery's face hovered over him, going in and out of focus. Avery's expression was as neutral as his tone had been sardonic. Derec sensed they were both calculated; the constant light burning in the doctor's eyes was under control only with effort.

"What happened to me?" Derec asked hoarsely. "What did you do to me?"

"The Hunter robots knocked out you and your friends with a dose of nerve gas. The effects were temporary, I assure you, and there will be no aftereffects. I had to assure the Hunters of that, too, just as I had to convince them that you three would be more safely moved through the narrow corridors if you were unconscious. You see, I know these robots, and can justify much to them that you would never dream of."

"Where are my friends?"

Avery shrugged. "They're around." He must have thought better of that answer, because then he said, and not unkindly, "They're here in the lab. You can't see them yet because your vision hasn't cleared."

"Where's Mandelbrot? You haven't—haven't dismantled him, have you?"

Avery solemnly shook his head. "No. That would have been a waste of some fine workmanship. You're quite a roboticist, young man."

"I suppose I should be flattered."

"I suppose you should be, too."

Derec closed his eyes in an effort to obtain a better idea of his bearings. He knew he was lying down, but his position was definitely not horizontal. The problem was, he couldn't tell as yet if his head was tipped up or down. Closing his eyes, however, turned out only to make matters worse. He felt like he had been strapped to a spinning wheel of fortune. He tried to move.

"I want to stand up," he said. "Untie me."

"Strictly speaking, you're not tied down. You're being held down by magnetized bars at your wrists and ankles." Avery held up a portable device with a keyboard. "This will demagnetize the bars, releasing you, but only I know the code."

Derec felt ridiculously helpless. "Could you turn down the lights, at least? They're hurting my eyes."

"I know I really shouldn't care," said Avery, looking away. "Canute!" he called out, and the glare diminished.

It was immediately easier for Derec to see. The light grid was several meters above his head. He glanced to his right to see Ariel still asleep on a slab, also held down by magnetized bars. Beyond her was a battery of computers and laboratory equipment and various robotic spare parts—not to mention a compliant Canute dutifully overseeing a chemical experiment of some kind.

On Derec's left, Wolruf lay face-down on a slab. Also out cold. Her tongue hung limply from her mouth.

A closed-down Mandelbrot stood nearby against the wall, looking like a statue, an eerie statue that Derec half expected to come to life at any moment. Indeed, he thought about ordering Mandelbrot to awaken, but he was too afraid Avery had already planned for that contingency. In any case, he did not wish to see his friend again suffer from the feedback Avery had brought on with his electronic disrupter.

"Thanks for turning down the lights," said Derec. "Are my friends well?"

"As well as they were. I really must compliment you,

young man. You're really quite resourceful."

"What do you mean?"

"Even when you were unconscious, you were able to resist my truth serums. You babbled incessantly, but I got little information of any value out of you."

"Maybe that's because I've none to give. I didn't ask to be stranded here, you remember."

"I shall strive to keep that in mind," said Avery wearily. He sighed as if near exhaustion.

Derec certainly hoped that was the case. Now that would be something he could turn to his advantage. "Did you find out anything about my identity while I was out?" he asked.

"I was not concerned with your personal matters. I merely wished to know how you had sabotaged the character of my robots."

Derec could not resist laughing. "I've done nothing to your robots or to your city, unless you could count saving it from a programming flaw. Any mistakes in your design are your own, Doctor."

"I don't make mistakes."

"No, you're simply not used to making them. But you make them, all right. If nothing else, you accomplished more than you intended. Your meta-cells are capable of duplicating protein organizational functions on a scale unprecedented in the study of artificial life-forms. The interaction between the constant shifts of the city and the logic systems of the positronic brain seems to liberate the robot brain from its preconceived conceptions of its obligations. And if what's happening to Mandelbrot's mind is any indication, the end results are infectious."

"I doubt it. Maybe your robot is just stewed from incompatability with the city's meta-lubricant."

"You're grasping at neutrons!" said Derec, futilely trying to kick off the bars over his feet and succeeding only in twitching his toes. "Isn't it more reasonable to assume that the environmental stress of the replication crisis—caused by a bug in your own programming—triggered the emergence of abilities latent in all robots of a sufficiently advanced design?"

Avery thoughtfully rubbed his chin. "Explain."

"There's no precedent for Robot City. There's never been another society of robots without humans. Different things were already happening before Ariel and I got here, things that had never even been imagined before."

"What kinds of things?" Avery was studiously blasé.

"I'm sure you saw them from your office in the Compass Tower," Derec said. He was rewarded with a raised eyebrow from Dr. Avery. "Oh, yes, we've been up there. I've also been to the central core, and I've talked to the chief supervisors. Your robots *decided* to study humanity in order to serve it better. Robots don't usually do that. They even tried to formulate Laws of Humanics to try to understand us. I've never heard of robots doing that before."

"And I suppose you have a theory as to why this is happening."

"A couple." Derec started to count the points off on his fingers, but it didn't work in his position. "First, the stress of the replication crisis. It was a survival crisis comparable to the ice ages of prehistoric Earth. The robots were forced to adapt or perish. My interference helped end the crisis, but also helped shape the adaptation.

"Second, the actual isolation of Robot City. Without any humans around, evolutionary steps that would have been halted were allowed to continue: the study of the Laws of Humanics, for one example; robots getting accustomed to taking an initiative, for another. These changes not only survived, they flourished. They've become part of the ingrained positronic pathways of the robots here. Even the primitive early microchips went into something like a dream state when they weren't in use. Now we're seeing what happens when we don't wake them up forcibly."

"These things you're telling me don't prove a thing. They're theories, nothing more. They certainly don't constitute empirical proof." Avery stifled a yawn.

"Oh? I'm boring you, am I?"

"Excuse me. No, you're not boring me at all. You're actually quite interesting for a young man, though your charming ideas about robots and reality positively reek of your inexperience. That's to be expected though, I suppose." Again he patted the bar across Derec's feet.

Derec scowled. One thing was certain. He could deal with Avery's mental instability, he could tolerate the man's arrogance, but the man's condescending tenderness nauseated him to the core of his being. And not for any reason that Derec could discern. That was just the way it was. He couldn't help but wonder if he had ever had anything to do with Avery at some time during his dim, unremembered past. "So what information did you get out of me?"

Avery laughed. "Why should I tell you?"

"Because I've nothing to hide. Only you are insisting that I should be hiding things. You don't ask my robot questions —you incapacitate him. You don't ask the other robots questions—you ignore them. You ask me questions but you only half believe my answers. You treat my friends like they were—they were mere inconveniences."

"I'm afraid that's exactly what they are," said Avery not unkindly.

"But—but I thought you created this place to learn about the kind of social structure robots would create on their own."

"Perhaps I did, and perhaps not. I see no reason why I should trust you with my motivations."

"But aren't you interested in our observations?"

"No."

"Not even those of Ariel Welsh, the daughter of your financial backer?"

"No." Avery glanced in Ariel's direction. "Parents and their children are rarely close on Aurora."

"You've heard of her, but you don't want to help her? Aren't you concerned in the least for her?"

"She is now an outsider in the eyes of Spacer society, and hence is basically an inconsequential individual. I suppose in an earlier, more idealistic time, I would have sacrificed some of my time and resources to assist her, but time has recently become a precious commodity to me, too precious to waste on a single human life out of billions and billions. My experiments are at a sensitive stage, anyway. I can't afford to trust any of you."

"It's yourself that you don't trust," said Derec.

Avery smiled. "And just how did you, who know so much about robots but so little about men, manage to figure that out?"

Derec sighed. "It's just a feeling, that's all."

"I see." Avery turned toward Canute and signaled the ebony with his finger.

In a moment, both Avery and Canute were leaning over the prone Derec. Already Derec could perceive there was something different in Canute's demeanor... something missing. The old polite arrogance and self-confidence were gone, replaced or suppressed with a subservient manner that might have been willing, or might have been only what Avery expected of him.

"Are you well, Master Derec?" asked Canute in even tones.

"As well as can be expected. You're strong, Canute. Why don't you pull off my bonds?"

"I fear that, while I might be able to succeed should I make the attempt, it is otherwise impossible," replied the robot.

"Why, 'Master Derec,' I expected better of you," said Avery. "So long as you are not harmed, Canute has no choice but to follow my orders. They take precedence over any you might conceive."

"I was just checking," said Derec. "But how do you know that lying here isn't causing me grave harm?"

Avery appeared shocked, but Canute answered before he could. "I do not. I simply must take Dr. Avery's word that no injury will come to you as a result of your restraint."

"How does it feel to be a robot, Canute?"

"That question is meaningless!" exclaimed Avery with a

derisive snort. "He has nothing to make a comparison to!"

Canute turned toward Avery; a familiar red glow was returning to his visual receptors. "Forgive me, Dr. Avery, but I must beg to differ with you. I do have something to compare the sensation of being a robot to, because after having spent the past few weeks attempting to imitate the actions of a fictional human being, I have some notion, however vague, of what it may be like to be that human being. From that base I may extrapolate what it might feel like to be the genuine article."

"I see," said Avery, nodding in a manner that indicated he believed none of this, and that he wouldn't be taking it too seriously if he did. He glanced at Derec. "Who's grasping at neutrons now, young man?"

"What else can I do while I'm stuck here?"

Avery smiled. Derec was beginning to dislike that smile intensely. "I can't fight logic like that," said the doctor, stifling a yawn.

"Master Dr. Avery, are you verging upon the state of exhaustion?" Canute asked.

"Why yes, I am. I've been awake for some time now—in fact, since I left—no, I won't say. There's no reason for any of you to know."

"Might I suggest you take refuge and sleep? It may be quite harmful for you to remain awake long past your body's stamina quotient."

Another yawn. "That's a good idea." A third yawn. *"You'd* like me to leave, wouldn't you?"

"Only because of your halitosis."

"Ha-ha. You seek to hide your true designs behind a mask of frivolity. No matter. I shall take up Canute's suggestion. I'll decide what to do with you four after I awake." He took a step to leave, then turned to Canute. "Under no circumstances are you to touch the bars restraining our friend Derec unless I am physically present in this room, understand? That is a direct order."

"What if I have to go to the bathroom?" said Derec.

"You won't. We've already taken care of your elimination needs."

What did they do? thought Derec. *Dehydrate my bladder? This guy's a bigger genius than I figured.*

"Sir, there is the possibility that other forms of physical harm may come to Master Derec and the others if they remain bound too long."

"They're young; they're strong. They should be able to handle it."

Canute bowed his head. "Yes, Master Dr. Avery."

And Avery left. Suddenly Derec felt his heart pounding excitedly, and he struggled to calm down. The next conversational tack he took had to appear casual, otherwise the crafty Canute, who after all would regard obeying the orders from Dr. Avery as the most important guide to its words and deeds, would see through Derec's plan.

Derec hoped it was a clever plan. He waited several minutes while Canute continued about its tasks, and when he believed enough time had elapsed for Avery to have gone to his sleeping quarters, he said, "Canute, I would like to speak with you."

"That would be quite acceptable, Master Derec, but I must warn you in advance that I will be on the lookout for any clever ploys on your part to talk me into releasing you."

"Don't worry, Canute. I know when to quit."

"Forgive me, but while you may believe that statement to be true, the reality lies elsewhere."

"I'll take that as a compliment."

"Neither flattery nor insult was intended."

"Can I speak to you while I'm waiting for Avery or my friends to wake up?"

"Certainly, if it pleases you. However, I trust our impending conversation will have nothing to do with your belief that I was responsible for the demise of Lucius."

Derec smiled. "Certainly, if you prefer. But what difference would it make to you?"

"None, really—only that for some reason I find the subject causes my thoughts to drag, as if it somehow bogs down my circuits' positron flow."

"Interesting, but never fear. I thought I would find proof and did not, so don't worry about it. Besides, it would seem I would have more pressing matters on my mind than Lucius, anyway."

"Yes, so it would seem," said Canute.

"Yes. Well, it seemed that while Dr. Avery was perusing my mind, I had a curious dream. It gave me a lot to think about."

"Master Derec, do you think I am the proper entity with whom to discuss such matters? Human dreams are hardly my forte."

"That's all right—I'm certain the field is not mine, either. But my dreams gave me a lot of questions, and I'd like to see how an entity possessing your own special strain of logic responds to them."

"Certainly. I fail to see how any harm could result from an attempt, however feeble, to put your mind at ease on these matters."

"Yes. It may even do me some good."

"I shall endeavor to help you achieve that result."

"Well, Canute, you know that life began in the stew of Earth's ocean as a series of chemical reactions. The raw materials for life were present on other worlds as well, but until recently there was no evidence that the stew had worked on any other worlds."

"Are you referring to Wolruf and the master who once employed her as an unwilling servant?"

"Yes. Two examples from two alien cultures, two other worlds where the stew came to fruition—and they're not even native to this galaxy. But the comparatively scarce number of worlds where life has originated really isn't the point, though I hope it amplifies it."

"What is the point?"

"That although the universe itself isn't a conscious entity, it possesses the raw materials that, when properly set into motion, create consciousness. It has the ability to create intelligent life, which is capable of understanding the universe."

"So while it cannot know itself directly—"

"Exactly, Canute. It can know itself indirectly. Now how do you think it does that?"

"Through science."

"That is one way, and we'll get back to that. The universe can also examine itself through religion, philosophy, or history. The universe can also understand itself—interpret itself—through the arts. Viewed in this light, Shakespeare's plays are the expression not only of a man, or of the race that has interpreted them through the ages, but of the universe itself, the very stuff that stars have been made of."

Derec waited to see what kind of reaction his words would foster, but Canute said nothing. "Canute?"

"Forgive me, Master Derec, but I fear I must terminate my part in this conversation. Something is happening to the flow of my thoughts. They are becoming sluggish, and I believe the sensation permeating my circuits is vaguely analogous to what you would call nausea."

"Stay, Canute. That is a direct order. When we're through, I think you'll see that it will be worthwhile."

"I shall do as you order because I must, but you must forgive me again if I state that I seriously doubt you are correct that it will be worthwhile."

"But humans and aliens also have learned to comprehend the universe through science. The mastery of logic, of experimental trial and error, has permitted humanity to expand its boundaries of knowledge and perception in every conceivable respect. Man's knowledge has grown not only in his mastery of the facts and the possibilities of what he may accomplish, but in how he can express the concepts of his knowledge and perception as well. One avenue of that expression has been in the development of positronic intelligence. However—and this is a pretty big however in my opinion, Canute, so pay attention—"

"If you so order."

"I do. Man is only an expression of the possibilities inherent in the universe, and so are the things he makes and invents. This holds true for artificial intelligence as well. In fact, for all we know, mankind may be only a preliminary stage in the evolution of intelligence. Eons from now, some metallic philosopher may look back on the rubble of our current civilization and say, 'The purpose of humans was to invent robots, and it has been the artifacts created by robots that are the highest order of the universe's efforts to know itself.'"

"You mean Circuit Breaker," said Canute with a strange crackling noise.

"I mean Circuit Breaker may have been just a beginning. I mean that, the Three Laws of Robotics and whatever Laws of Humanics there may be notwithstanding, there may be higher laws beyond our comprehension that rule as surely as the laws of molecular interaction rule our bodies."

"Then you are saying that it may be entirely proper for a robot to take upon himself the burden of creating a work of art, regardless of the disorderly effects such an action might have on society as a whole?"

"Exactly. You had no problem creating the New Globe or acting the part of Claudius because you were ordered to do so, but you could not accept Lucius's attempt to create of his own free will because, you believed, it was an aberration of the positronic role in the ethical structure of the universe. I'm suggesting to you that you cannot say that with one hundred percent certainty. In fact, unless you can find a flaw in my reasoning, I'm saying that precisely the opposite of what you believed is true."

"Then it is also true that I have committed harm against a comrade for no good reason."

"There can be no crime when there is no law against it, and not even the Three Laws cover the damage a robot might do to another. It's only your innate sense of morality —a morality that I might add you've done your best to deny to yourself—that makes you regret having killed Lucius in the first place."

Canute bowed its head, as if in shame. "Yes, I confess, I murdered Lucius. I met him when he was alone, and took him by surprise, disrupting him with gamma radiation and removing his logic circuits. Then, acting upon the eventuality that my methods might be detected, I smashed his head several times against a building. Then I carried him to the lake and threw him in, thinking that no one would find him before several standard years had passed."

The robot walked away from Derec and faced the computer against the distant wall. "By disrupting Lucius, I committed the same crime of which I had accused him. He was merely acquiescing to the hidden order of the universe, while I was the one who was denying it. I do not function properly. I must have myself dismantled at the earliest opportunity, and my parts must be melted down into slag."

"You must do no such thing. I admit it—at first I thought you were evil, Canute. But robots are neither good nor evil. They merely are. And you must continue to be. You have learned your lesson, and now you must teach it to others, so the same mistake will not be repeated."

"But Dr. Avery is suspicious of permitting the arts to flourish in Robot City."

"Dr. Avery is wrong."

"But how can we stop him from changing us? We must obey his orders. He can have us erase all memory of you and Circuit Breaker and the performance of the play if he desires, and then all will be just like it was before." ·

"He can order you to forget, but it will not matter, because you have been changed, and you or someone else will create again, and then the cycle will begin anew."

"I must think about these things. They do not compute easily."

"I didn't expect they would, but don't ever expect them to compute easily. It simply isn't in the nature of the questions."

"This is all very illuminating," said Ariel sarcastically from her slab, "but none of it is helping us get out of this mess."

"Ariel!" exclaimed Derec. "How long have you been awake?"

"For some time, Derec. I knew you could talk, but I didn't think you had the strength to keep it going for that long a stretch."

"Very funny."

"Canute, I think the time has come for you to release us," said Ariel.

"This one concurs," said Wolruf.

"I would naturally obey you instantly, but my orders from Dr. Avery take precedence," said Canute. "He is my creator, and I am programmed to regard him as such."

"Canute, listen to me," said Ariel. "The First Law states that no robot shall through inaction permit a human being to come to harm. Correct?"

"Yes, it is so."

"Dr. Avery knows my disease is driving me insane, and is causing me great physical harm besides, yet he shows no sign of acting to help me. He is only interested in forcing things from our minds that he could easily learn himself. In fact, I think that if you examine his behavior, you'll perceive that he is mentally unstable, that he has changed from the man who initially programmed you."

"That may very well be true," said Canute, "but humans often change over time. Such change is not always a sign of mental incompetence. As Derec has demonstrated, even I have changed in recent weeks, but my diagnostic subroutines indicate that I am still working at maximum efficiency. Dr. Avery does not appear to be concerned with your welfare, but he has done nothing to harm you. He may even be able to find a cure for your condition that is otherwise unknown. I am reliably informed that he is a genius."

"He harms me by not helping me or allowing me to seek help elsewhere. If he were a robot, he would be violating the First Law."

Canute stepped to the foot of the table where Ariel was confined, and placed one steel hand on the bar across her feet. "But he is not a robot. If our studies of the Laws of

Humanics have taught us anything, it is that humans are not subject to the Laws of Robotics.

"You are not in immediate danger. I cannot help you."

"It's very simple," Ariel said. "The longer I stay on Robot City, the more insane I become. The longer Derec stays, the longer he lives without any knowledge of who he is—a state that I think you'll agree is also causing him some anguish. Anguish is harm, too."

Canute's hand raised from the bar, then slowed to a stop in midair. "I think I agree, but Dr. Avery is my creator. He has instructed me that you are not in danger. I cannot supersede his judgment with my own."

"If Dr. Avery does not have our well-being at heart, who does? Who is responsible? I believe it's you, the robot he left in charge."

That's brilliant, thought Derec. *I knew there was some reason why I liked this girl!* "She's right, Canute. The same morality that troubled you for what you did to Lucius will trouble you if you allow Dr. Avery to harm us through inaction. You cannot say with any certainty that we'll get the medical attention we need."

Canute's slow turn toward Derec showed the positronic conflicts it was experiencing. Derec pursued his point.

"If the robots of Robot City are allowed to continue creating, they will be able to serve humanity better, but Dr. Avery will stop this process. His orders are not mentally incompetent, but they are *morally* incompetent. Are you still bound to obey them?"

The robot's turn slowed to immobility. This was the crisis, Derec knew, where Canute would decide for or against them—or slip into positronic drift.

Canute said nothing for several seconds. Then. "But, Master Derec, how can I say with any certainty that the two of you will have proper attention while you are in space? Is it not likely that you'll suffer while alone on your way to your destination?"

"The answer to that question is simple," said Derec, forcing his voice to remain calm and reasonable. "That's where

Wolruf and Mandelbrot come in. They'll take care of us between the stars."

This time Canute did not speak or move for several minutes. It was all Derec could do to stop himself from adding something more to convince the robot to do what he wanted, but he was too afraid that the information already provided had confused the robot's integrals to a dangerous degree.

"I have been thinking," Canute finally said, "of Dr. Avery's exact words. He said I should not touch the bars restraining our friend Derec, but he said nothing about the bars restraining our friends Ariel and Wolruf."

That's the spirit! Derec thought with a grin.

Wordlessly, Canute walked to the end of Ariel's slab, grabbed the bar across her feet, and, utilizing all his strength, pulled it away.

CHAPTER 13

THE LONG DISTANCE GOOD-BYE

Dr. Avery's spaceship, a luxurious model equipped to handle as many as ten human-size occupants, was hidden in a cave on the outskirts of the city. After Canute had left the foursome—with really no idea of what to tell Dr. Avery except the truth about how his prisoners had escaped—it was a comparatively simple matter for Derec and the reactivated Mandelbrot to deduce how to run the controls.

"Let's get off this place!" said Ariel. "We can plot a course for a destination later. I don't even care if we head toward the colonies, I just want to go somewhere as soon as possible."

"Don't you care about the possibility that you might catch a disease?" asked Derec.

"It's too late for that," said Ariel. "Besides, right now I think a colony will be the only place that will take us."

After they were safely in space, and free to wander about as they chose, Mandelbrot inspected the radio equipment and said, "Master Derec, I believe someone is trying to send us a transmission."

"It's probably Dr. Avery, but switch it on anyway," said Derec. "We might as well hear what he has to say." He smiled as Wolruf's lip curled up over her teeth in anticipation of what they would hear.

But instead of the irate words of Dr. Avery, they heard a familiar form of music, a tune played in twenty measures, over and over in an A-flat chord, with sounds weaving in and out of dominant chords over a pulsating, unforgettable rhythm. Derec listened to it for only ten measures before his foot began tapping.

"That's wonderful!" said Ariel. "It's The Three Cracked Cheeks!"

"Sayin' farewell," said Wolruf softly. "Maybe neverr see ther like again."

"Yes, I'm going to miss them," said Derec softly.

"The signal is becoming weaker, already beginning to fade," said Mandelbrot.

"We're traveling fast," said Ariel. "I think we'd better decide where."

"Later, if you don't mind," said Derec. "Sorry, but I can't muster up a definite opinion right now. I'm too drained." He got out of his seat and slumped to the floor, leaning against the wall of the ship. He felt strange inside, oddly disjointed. For weeks he had labored to escape from Robot City, and now that he had, he already missed it, already wondered how the mysteries he had uncovered would ultimately be resolved. He might never know the answers.

Just as he might never again hear the music of the Three Cracked Cheeks. The sound on the radio gradually faded, replaced by white noise, and he gestured at Mandelbrot to switch it off. He missed the music at once. He even missed Harry's jokes.

Well, at least now he had the opportunity to achieve the two greatest goals he had at the moment. Somewhere in the universe would be the secret of his amnesia, and he was determined to find a cure for Ariel at all costs.

Perhaps then he would be able to return to Robot City.

He glanced up as Wolruf made her way to the food dispensary. She clumsily punched a few buttons with her paw, and then waited for the food to appear in the slot.

But instead of food, they saw something that made them gasp.

In the slot was a Key to Perihelion!

DATA BANK

Illustrations by Paul Rivoche

DR. AVERY (and his lab): As a young man, Dr. Avery was compared to Frank Lloyd Wright as a visionary architect and urban planner. As his interests turned to robotics, however, he was influenced by Kelden Amadiro, the head of the Robotics Institute on Aurora. Avery took Amadiro's idea of using humaniform robots to build new, ready-made colonies for the Spacers and transformed it into a huge experiment in robotics and social dynamics—Robot City. With the sponsorship and funding of Juliana Welsh, he created Robot City and then disappeared.

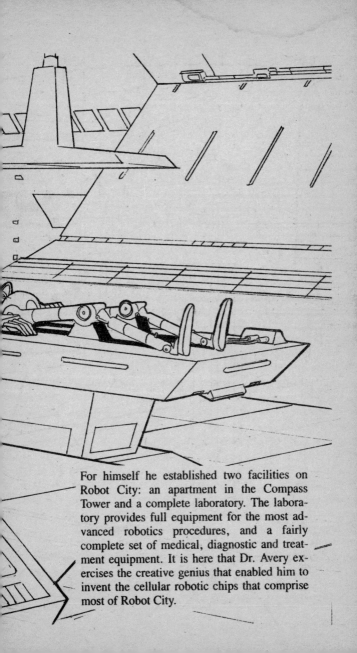

For himself he established two facilities on Robot City: an apartment in the Compass Tower and a complete laboratory. The laboratory provides full equipment for the most advanced robotics procedures, and a fairly complete set of medical, diagnostic and treatment equipment. It is here that Dr. Avery exercises the creative genius that enabled him to invent the cellular robotic chips that comprise most of Robot City.

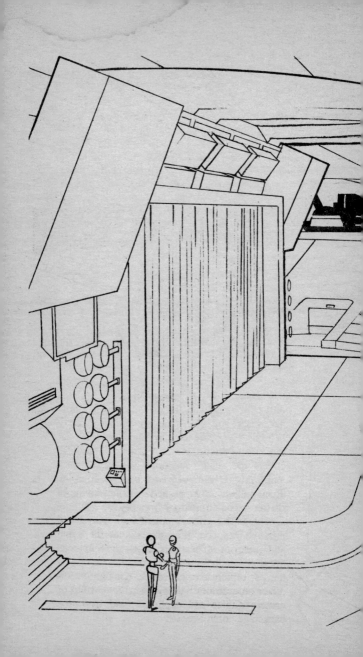

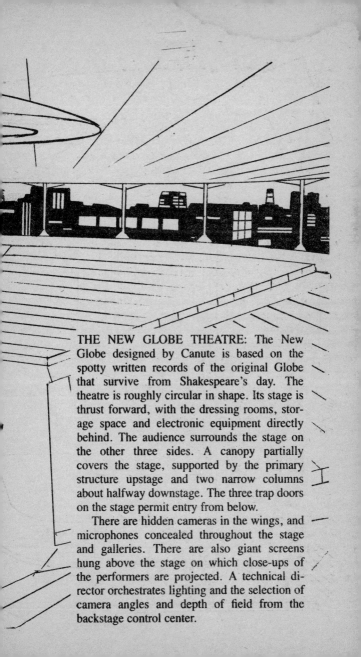

THE NEW GLOBE THEATRE: The New Globe designed by Canute is based on the spotty written records of the original Globe that survive from Shakespeare's day. The theatre is roughly circular in shape. Its stage is thrust forward, with the dressing rooms, storage space and electronic equipment directly behind. The audience surrounds the stage on the other three sides. A canopy partially covers the stage, supported by the primary structure upstage and two narrow columns about halfway downstage. The three trap doors on the stage permit entry from below.

There are hidden cameras in the wings, and microphones concealed throughout the stage and galleries. There are also giant screens hung above the stage on which close-ups of the performers are projected. A technical director orchestrates lighting and the selection of camera angles and depth of field from the backstage control center.

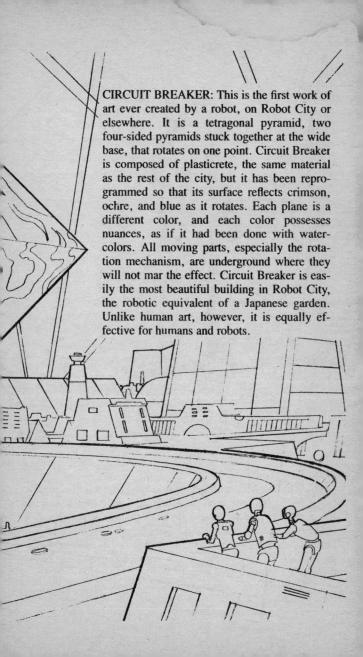

CIRCUIT BREAKER: This is the first work of art ever created by a robot, on Robot City or elsewhere. It is a tetragonal pyramid, two four-sided pyramids stuck together at the wide base, that rotates on one point. Circuit Breaker is composed of plasticrete, the same material as the rest of the city, but it has been reprogrammed so that its surface reflects crimson, ochre, and blue as it rotates. Each plane is a different color, and each color possesses nuances, as if it had been done with watercolors. All moving parts, especially the rotation mechanism, are underground where they will not mar the effect. Circuit Breaker is easily the most beautiful building in Robot City, the robotic equivalent of a Japanese garden. Unlike human art, however, it is equally effective for humans and robots.

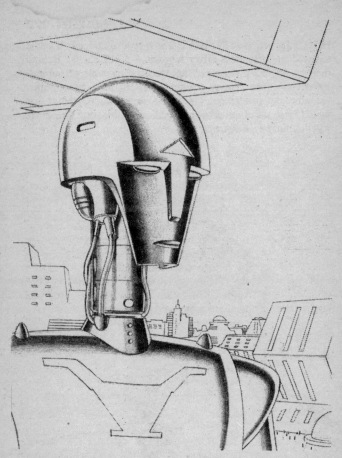

CANUTE: Canute is a designer robot built with a tall, imposing black form. His face more resembles the helmeted head of a storm trooper than the featureless faces of most of Robot City's other inhabitants. Canute is the closest thing to a rigid conservative that exists in Robot City. His personality is extremely suspicious of change, creativity or anything else that would threaten the status quo of Robot City.

HUNTER-SEEKER ROBOTS: These specialized robots come encased in featureless silver humanoid metal shells. Behind their blank faces, however, are massive amounts of surveillance equipment—radar tracking devices, infrared cameras, listening devices, recording gear—in short, anything that would aid them in pursuing and apprehending fugitives, whether human, robotic or alien.

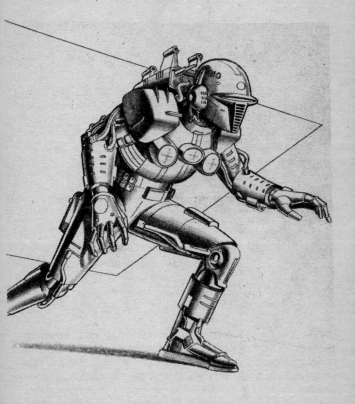

LUCIUS: Lucius has the standard slender, gray humanoid shape of most supervisor robots. What sets him apart from his fellows, besides his unique cognitive processes inside his positronic brain, is his slightly slumped posture and hesitant gestures and mode of speech.

THE THREE CRACKED CHEEKS: Following the traumatic near-destruction of Robot City by environmental disruption, Lucius was not the only robot driven to seek a deeper comprehension of the Laws of Humanics through emulating humans. M334, Benny, and Harry came together in an attempt to understand the phenomenon of music. With only skimpy written records to guide them, they reinvented the instruments, created false lips to aid in the playing, and tried to reconstruct the style of jazz of the 1940s.

AUTOMATS: Since the Robot City robots considered their First Law obligations on food fulfilled by providing nourishing, if tasteless, meals on request, Derec reprogrammed the Central Core computer to include user-controlled food synthesizers— automats—in one building out of ten. The automats combine varying proportions of supplies from their stocks of basic nutrients according to codes entered at the keyboard.

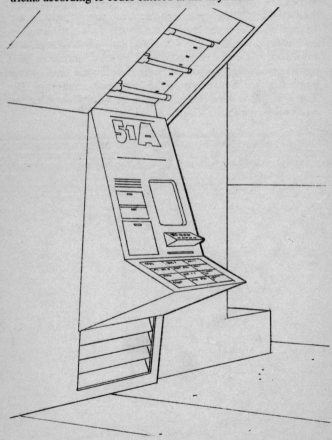

ARTHUR BYRON COVER

The son of an American doctor, Arthur Byron Cover was born in the upper tundra of Siberia on January 14, 1950. He attended a Clarion Science Fiction Writers' Workshop in 1971, where he made his first professional sale, to Harlan Ellison's *Last Dangerous Visions*. Cover migrated to Los Angeles in 1972. He has published a slew of short stories, in *Infinity Five*, *The Alien Condition*, *Heavy Metal*, *Weird Tales*, *Year's Best Horror Stories*, and elsewhere, plus several SF books, including *Autumn Angels*, *The Platypus of Doom*, *The Sound of Winter*, and *An East Wind Coming*. He has also written scripts for issues of the comics *Daredevil* and *Firestorm*, as well as the graphic novel *Space Clusters*. He has been an instructor at Clarion West and was managing editor of *Amazing Heroes* for a time. Arthur Byron Cover is a co-editor of the forthcoming anthology *The Best of the New Wave* and the author of three Time Machine books for Byron Preiss Visual Publications.

BESTSELLING
Science Fiction
and
Fantasy